LIGHT LIFTING

LIGHT
LIFTING

(stories)

Alexander MacLeod

BIBLIOASIS

FIRST EDITION
Second printing, October 2010

Library and Archives Canada Cataloguing in Publication

MacLeod, Alexander, 1972-
    Light lifting / Alexander MacLeod.

ISBN 978-1-897231-94-4

    I. Title.

PS8625.L445L54 2010   C813'.6   C2010-904592-0

  Canada Council for the Arts — **Conseil des Arts du Canada**   **ONTARIO ARTS COUNCIL** — **CONSEIL DES ARTS DE L'ONTARIO**

Canadian Heritage — Patrimoine canadien   **NOVA SCOTIA** Tourism, Culture and Heritage

Biblioasis acknowledges the ongoing financial support of the Government of Canada through The Canada Council for the Arts, Canadian Heritage, the Book Publishing Industry Development Program (BPIDP); and the Government of Ontario through the Ontario Arts Council. The author would like to thank the Canada Council and the Nova Scotia Ministry of Tourism and Culture for their financial support.

PRINTED AND BOUND IN CANADA

FSC
Mixed Sources
Cert no. SW-COC-001271
© 1996 FSC

Contents

For Crystal

Miracle Mile

This was the day after Mike Tyson bit off Evander Holyfield's ear. You remember that. It was a moment in history – not like Kennedy or the planes flying into the World Trade Center – not up at that level. This was something lower, more like Ben Johnson, back when his eyes were that thick, yellow colour and he tested positive in Seoul after breaking the world record in the hundred. You might not know exactly where you were standing or exactly what you were doing when you first heard about Tyson or about Ben, but when the news came down, I bet it stuck with you. When Tyson bit off Holyfield's ear, that cut right through the everyday clutter. All the papers and the television news shows ran the exact same pictures of Tyson standing there in his black trunks with the blood in his mouth. It seemed like everything else that happened that day had to be related back to this, back to Mike and what he had done. You have to remember, this was before Tyson got the tattoo on his face and the rematch with Holyfield was supposed to be his big comeback, a chance to go straight and be legitimate again. Nobody thinks about that now. Now, the only thing you see when you look back is Mike moving in for the kill, the way his cheek brushes up almost intimately against Evander's face just before he breaks all the way through and gives in to his rawest impulse. Then the tendons in his neck bulge out and his eyes pop wide open and his teeth come grinding down.

Burner and I were stuck in another hotel room, watching the sports highlights churn it around and around, the same thirty-second clip of the fight. It was like watching the dryer roll clothes. Cameras showed it from different angles and at different speeds and there were lots of close-ups of Evander's mangled head and the chunk of flesh lying there in the middle of the ring. Commentators took turns explaining what was happening and what it all meant.

The cleaning lady had already come and gone and now we had two perfectly made double beds, a fresh set of towels and seven empty hours before it would be time for us to go. We just sat there, side by side, beds three feet apart, perched on top of our tight blankets like a pair of castaways on matching rafts drifting in the same current. Mike kept coming at us through the screen. You know how it gets. If you look at the same pictures long enough even the worst things start to feel too familiar, even boring. I turned the TV off but the leftover buzz hanging in the air still hurt my eyes.

"Enough?" I asked, though I knew there'd be no response.

Burner didn't say anything. His eyes were kind of glossed over and he just sat there staring straight into the same dark place where the picture used to be. He'd been fading in and out for the last few hours.

If I have learned one thing through all this, it's that you have to let people do what they're going to do. Everybody gets ready in their own way. Some guys play their music loud, some say their prayers and some can't keep anything down and they're always running to the toilet. Burner wasn't like that. He liked to keep it quiet in the morning, to just sit around and watch mindless TV so he could wander off in his mind and come back anytime he liked. One minute, he could be sitting there, running his mouth off about nothing, and then for no reason, he'd

zone out and go way down into himself and stay there perfectly silent for long stretches, staring off to the side like he
was trying to remember the name of someone he should
really know.

It didn't bother me. Over the years, Burner and I had been
in plenty of hotel rooms together and by now we had our act
down. I didn't mind the way he folded his clothes into perfect
squares and put them into the hotel dresser drawers even
when we were staying a single night, and I don't think he
cared about the way I dumped my bag into a pile in the
corner and pulled out the things I needed. You have to let
people do what they do. When you get right down to it, even
the craziest ritual and the wildest superstition are based on
somebody's version of real solid logic.

After fifteen minutes of nothing, Burner said "I'm not
going to wear underwear."

He was all bright and edgy now and his eyes started jumping around the room. He licked his top lip every few seconds
with just the tip of his tongue darting out.

"No, not going to wear underwear."

He nodded his head this second time, as if, at last, some
big decision had finally been made and he was satisfied with
the result.

I didn't say anything. When he was this far down,
Burner didn't need anybody to keep up the other end of
the conversation.

"You feel faster without underwear, you know. But I only
do it once or twice a year. Only for the big ones."

That was it. A second later he was gone again, back below
the surface, off to the side.

I turned away from him and punched a slightly bigger
dent into my pillow so there'd be more room for my head. I
knew there was no chance, but I still closed my eyes and tried

to sleep. The alarm on the table said it was 12:17 and no matter what you do you can't trick those early afternoon numbers. Every red minute was going to leak out of that clock like water coming through the ceiling, building up nice and slow before releasing even one heavy drop. I waited, and I am sure I counted to sixty-five, but when I looked back 12:18 still hadn't come down. I flopped over onto my back and looked at the little stalagmites in the stucco. I thought about those little silver star-shaped things that are supposed to go off if there's a fire.

I'll tell you what I was wearing: my lucky Pogues T-shirt for the warm-up, a ratty Detroit Tigers baseball cap, the same pair of unwashed shorts that had worked okay for me last week and a pair of black track pants that weren't made of cotton, but some kind of space-age, breathable, moisture-wicking material. On my left foot, I had one expensive running shoe that Adidas had given me for free. Its partner was on the floor beside the bed and I had about a dozen other pairs still wrapped in tissue paper and sitting in their boxes at home. My right foot was bare because I had just finished icing it for the third time that morning. The wet ziplock bag of shrunken hotel ice cubes was slumped at the end of my bed, melting, and my messed-up Achilles was still bright red from the cold. I could just start to feel the throb coming back into it.

I meshed my fingers together on my chest and tried to make them go up and down as slowly as possible. It was coming and we were waiting for it. The goal now was to do absolutely nothing and let time flow right over us. It would have been impossible to do less and still be alive. I felt like one of the bodies laid out in a funeral home, waiting for the guests to arrive. You couldn't put these things off forever. Eventually it had to end. In a couple hours, some guy dressed all in white would say "Take your marks." Then, one second later, there'd be the gun.

I DON'T KNOW how much time passed before Burner hopped off his bed like he was in a big rush. He went around our room cranking open all the taps until we had all five running full blast. There were two in the outside sink, the one by the big mirror with all the lights around it, two in the bathroom sink and one big one for the tub. Burner had them all going at once. Water running down the drain was supposed to be a very soothing sound that helped you focus and visualize everything more clearly. This was all part of thinking like a champion. At least that's what the sports psychology guys said and Burner thought they were right on.

There was a lot of steam at first and we had our own little cloud forming up around the ceiling, but after a while, after we'd used up all the hot water for the entire hotel, the mist cleared and there was only the *shhhhhhh* sound of the water draining away. It was actually kind of nice. You could just try and put yourself inside that sound and it would carry you some place else, maybe all the way to the ocean.

When Burner surfaced for the last time, when he came back for good, he looked over at me and said, "Do you know what your problem is?"

I took a breath and waited for it.

"You can't see," he said.

"You don't have vision. If you want to do this right, you need to be able to see how it's going to happen before it actually happens. You have to be in there, in the race, a hundred times in your head before you really do it."

I nodded because I had to. This season, unlike all the others, Burner was in the position to give advice. For the last three years I had beat him from Vancouver to Halifax and back a hundred times and in all that time I had never said a thing about it. He'd never even been close. But this year – the year of the trials, the year when they picked the team for the World Championships and they were finally going to fund all the spots – this was the year when Burner finally had it all put together at the right time and I couldn't get anything going. For the last eight weeks, in eight different races in eight different cities, he'd come flying by me in the last one-fifty and there was nothing I could do about it.

I don't know where it came from or how he did it, but Burner had it all figured out. For the last year he'd been on this crazy diet where it seemed like he only ate green vegetables – just broccoli and spinach and Brussel sprouts all the time. And he hadn't had a drop of alcohol or a cup of coffee in months. He said he had gone all the way over to the straight edge and that he would never allow another bad substance into his body again. He broke up with his girlfriend and quit going out, even to see a movie. He drank this special decaffeinated green tea and he shaved his head right down to the nut. I think he weighed around 125 or 130. He practiced some watered-down version of Buddhist mysticism and he was interested in yoga and always reading these books with titles like "Going for Gold!: Success the Kenyan Way," or "Unlocking Your Inner Champion." Whatever he was doing, it was working. Out of all that mess, he had found some little kernel of truth and now he was putting it into action.

"The secret is to think about nothing," he said.

"Just let it all hang out. Mind blank and balls to the wall. That's all there is. Keep it simple, stupid. Be dumb. Just run."

IT'S HARD TO TELL anybody what it's really like. Most people have seen too many of those CBC profiles that run during the Olympics, the ones with the special theme music and the

torch and all those fuzzy soft camera shots that make everyone look so young and radiantly healthy. I used to think –
everybody used to think – they were going to make one of
those little movies about me, but I know now it's never going
to happen. It's timing. Everything is timing. I was down
when I needed to be up. If we were both at our best, if Burner
and I were both going at it at the top of our games, he would
lose. We both knew this. My best times were ahead of his, but
I was far from my best now. There were even high-school kids
now, coming up from behind and charging hard. I don't
really know what I was waiting for in that room. I might cut
the top five, maybe, but I knew I wouldn't be close enough to
be in the photograph when the first guy crossed the line. It
wasn't really competition anymore. For me, this was straight
autopilot stuff, going through the motions and following my
own ritual right through to the end.

"What about Bourque?" I said.

This was the last part for Burner. I'd say the name of a guy
who was going to be there with us and he would describe the
guy's weaknesses. Burner needed to do this, needed to know
exactly why the others could not win. There were maybe
ten people like us in the whole country, and no more than
five or six who had a real shot at making the team, but
Burner needed to hate all of them. That was how he worked.
I couldn't care less, but I did my part. I kept my eyes on the
sprinklers and didn't even look at him. I just released the
words into the air. I let Bourque's name float away.

"Bourque? What is Bourque? A 3:39, 3:40 guy at the top
end of his dreams. We won't even see him. Too slow. Period.
We won't even see him."

"Dawson is supposed to be here," I said. He was the next
guy on the list.

"He ran 3:37.5 at NC's last month."

"Got no guts," Burner sort of snorted it.

"Dawson needs everything to be perfect. He needs a rabbit and a perfectly even pace and he needs there to be sunshine and no wind. He can run, no doubt, but he can't race. If you shake him up and throw any kind of hurt into him, he'll just fold. Guy's got tons of talent, but he's a coward. You know that, Mikey. Everybody knows that about Dawson. Even Dawson knows it, deep down. If somebody puts in a 57 second 400 in the middle of it, Dawson will be out the back end and he'll cry when it's over. He will actually cry. You will see the tears running down his face."

"Marcotte will take it out hard right from the gun," I said. "He'll open in 56 and then just try and hold on. He's crazy and he will never quit. There's no limit to how much that guy can hurt."

"But he can't hold it. You know how it'll be. Just like last week and the week before. It'll be exactly the same. Marcotte will blow his load too soon and we'll come sailing by with 300 to go. If we close in 42, he'll have nothing in the tank. He'll collapse and fall over at the finish line and somebody will have to carry him away."

THAT'S HOW WE TALKED most of the time. The numbers meant more than the words and the smaller numbers meant more than the bigger ones. It was like we belonged to our own little country and we had this secret language that almost nobody else understood. Almost nobody can tell you the real difference between 3:36 and 3:39. Almost nobody understands that there's something in there, something important and significant, just waiting to be released out of that space between the six and the nine. Put it this way: if you ever wanted to cross over that gap, if you ever wanted to see what it was like on the other side, you would need to change your entire life and get rid of almost everything else. You have to make choices: you can't run and be an astronaut. Can't run and have a full-time job. Can't run and have a girlfriend who doesn't run. When I stopped going to church or coming home for holidays, my mother used to worry that I was losing my balance, but I never met a balanced guy who ever got anything done. There's nothing new about this stuff. You have to sign the same deal if you want to be good – I mean truly good – at anything. Burner and I, and all those other guys, we understood this. We knew all about it. Every pure specialist is the same way so either you know what I am talking about or you do not.

"In the end, it's going to come back to Graham," I said. I'd been saving his name for last.

"Graham," Burner repeated it back to me.

"Graham, Graham, Graham, Graham."

It sounded almost like a spell or a voodoo curse, but what else could you say? We both knew there was no easy answer for Graham.

WHEN WE WERE KIDS in high school, back when we first joined the club and started training together, Burner and I used to race the freight trains through the old Michigan central railway tunnel. It was one of those impossible dangerous things that only invincible high school kids even try: running in the dark, all the way from Detroit to Windsor, underneath the river. When I think back, I still get kind of quaky and I can't believe we got away untouched. It didn't work out like that for everyone. Just a few years ago, a kid in the tunnel got sucked under one of those big red CP freighters and when they found him his left arm and his left leg had been cut right off. Somehow he lived, and everybody thought there must have been some kind of divine intervention. The doctors managed to reattach his arm and I think he got a state-of-the-art prosthetic leg paid for by the War Amps. The papers tried to turn it into a feel good piece, but all I could think about was how hard it would be for that kid to go through the rest of his life with that story stuck to him and the consequences of it so clear to everybody else.

Burner and I used to race the trains at night from the American side, under the river, and up through the other opening into the CP railyard, over by Wellington Avenue, where all the tracks bundle up and braid together. At that time, before the planes flew into the World Trade Center, there weren't any real border guards or customs officers or police posted on the rail tunnel. They just had fences. On the American side you had to climb over and on the Canadian side someone had already snipped a hole through the links and you could just walk. The train tunnel is twice as long as the one they use for the cars and I think we had it paced out at around two and a half miles or about fifteen minutes of hard blasting through the dark, trying not to trip over the switches or the broken ties or the ten thousand rats that live down there.

We'd drive Burner's car over to the American side, we'd hop the fence and then we'd just watch and wait for about fifteen minutes, trying to estimate how long it would be before the next train set out. We always went one guy at a time because there wasn't enough space between the side of the track and the wall of the tunnel and you couldn't risk getting tangled up. It was pitch black in there so we took these little flashlights that we wouldn't turn on until we were inside and even then you could only get a quick look at where you were and where you were headed. Once, I remember that Burner tried to tape one of those lights to his head so he could be like a miner and see everything more clearly, but he said that the light wouldn't stay where he needed it and that he had to rip it off after only a few steps.

When you think about what could have happened but didn't, it makes you wonder why we weren't more strategic or careful. We should have timed everything right down to the second, but back then it seemed so easy. We'd crouch down in the shadows beside the tunnel and then if everything looked okay, we'd shake hands and say something like "see you on the other side." Then the guy going second, the guy left behind, would count it down – three, two, one, go – and that would be it. The first guy would just take off.

We were always good runners, but ninety percent of racing the trains is just learning to deal with straight fear and the sensation you get from that hot surge of adrenaline flowing through you. It was all about going forward and just trying to stay up on your feet. If you did go down and you felt your leg brush against that damp fur of a rat or you caught your arm on some chunk of metal or got scraped up against the exposed wall of the tunnel, there was no time to even think about it. You just got up as quickly as you could and even though you could feel your pulse beating through an open cut and you might have wrenched your ankle pretty bad, you still had to go on as if everything was working perfectly according to plan.

It wasn't really racing at all. There's no way to actually win in a contest like that and you could never go head-to-head with the trains. This was more about just trying to stay ahead and that's something completely different. When they set off and they're just chugging out of the gate, those trains look slow and heavy and it seems like it should be easy to stay out front, especially when you're working with such a big head start. It doesn't work like that though. The trains pick up their momentum on the way down into the tunnel. They used to say that once you were in there running, if you ever heard the train coming up from behind, or if you even just caught the sound of that first echo, then that meant you had something like three minutes before it caught up and pulled you under. The other thing they always talked about was the light. They said that if the light ever touched you, if that big glare of the freighter ever landed right on you, then that was supposed to be the end. By that time the rig would be going too fast and even if he saw you the engineer wouldn't have time to shut everything down and stop. That's what happened to the kid who lost his arm and leg. By the time they radioed and got the paramedics and the stretchers all the way down there, the kid nearly bled to death in the dark. Then they had to go searching for his missing limbs and I guess they found one on the track and the other one, I think it was the leg, caught up underneath the train. Even after all that, he somehow pulled through.

Nothing ever happened to me. I must have run the tunnel half a dozen times, but I never heard or saw the train and the only thing that ever pushed me along was the need to get out. It just kept you going faster than you thought you could go and it kept you rolling right up until you felt the ground leaning up again, climbing out. In the dark, just that little shift in the angle of the earth under your feet would be enough to tell you that you were getting closer and you'd probably make it.

The worst time was the last time. It was my turn to go first and when I came through I was so messed up I knew I would never do it again. As soon as I made it out, I kind of collapsed off to the side, just one step beyond the tunnel. I must have fallen two or three times in there and I had a pretty nasty gash oozing down the front of my shin. I don't know why, but when I got out, I started throwing up and I couldn't make it stop. I thought I might pass out because I couldn't get a clean breath and my stomach was kind of convulsing and dry-heaving. My vision went all blurry and I couldn't see anything.

I was laying there in the scrub grass beside the tunnel, kind of curled up in the fetal position when I heard it – that long slow regular blast of the train. Usually Burner and I left a five minute gap between the first guy and the next guy and I was sure that much time had already passed. When I heard the horn again, I knew I'd been waiting too long. There was nothing I could do so I just pulled myself up and tried to peek around the corner of the concrete as best I could. I kept staring down into the dark and I was shaking and shivering now because I was so scared and the sweat was turning cold on my skin. I wasn't sure if I should try and find some official person and tell them to radio in and watch for Burner, but there was no one around. I was actually hoping that he'd been caught on the other side, or that he'd chickened out, or come to his senses. I didn't want to think about the other possibility but it still came flashing into my head. For one second I imagined how even at top speed, there would still have to be this one moment, just before the full impact, when Burner would feel only the beginning of it, just that slight little nudge of cold metal pressing up against his skin.

When I heard the sound of his feet banging on the gravel, coming closer, I thought I must have been making it up. I couldn't see anything, but I stood in the opening and waved my light around anyway, shouting his name. For a second I thought I could just make him out in the distance, maybe a hundred yards away but then the sound of the train blast rose up again and the whole rig came rolling around the last corner of the tunnel. I saw the big round light and it touched me and filled up the whole space, illuminating everything. I put my hand up like you do when you're trying to block out the sun and I saw him. Burner was there charging toward me, the only dark space in front of the light. He had this long line of spit hanging out of his mouth like a dog and the look on his face wasn't fear but something more like rage. The gap kept closing and it seemed to me like the big light was almost pushing him out. I emptied out my lungs yelling up against that bigger noise. I said "Come on, come on," and I waved my whole arm in a big circle, as if I could scoop out the space between us and reel him in.

In the end, it wasn't as close as it seemed. Burner came up and around the corner and he kind of ran me over as I tried to catch him. We had about ten or fifteen seconds to spare before the train came roaring through and that was enough time for us to take off and scramble through the hole in the fence. We knew they'd be making their calls and trying to track us down so we spent the next half hour running and hiding behind a few dumpsters and trying to make our way back to my car. We never had any time to talk about it until later that night when it became, like everything else in our pasts, a kind of joke. We called it "The night Burner pulled a train out of his ass."

But that's the image I keep of him – Burner running in the light and getting away. That's the one I keep. For those few seconds, he was like one of those fugitives trying to break out of prison and they just couldn't catch him. The train kept coming down on him like some massive predator and he shouldn't have had a chance, but he was like that one stupid gazelle on the nature show, the one who somehow gets away even though the cheetahs or lions or hyenas should already be feasting. Burner was one of those fine-limbed lucky bastards, but he was still here and his life, like mine, kept rolling along, filling in all this extra time.

WE GOT OUR STUFF TOGETHER and left the hotel at around four o'clock with our bags slung over our shoulders. We took a shuttle bus, one of those big coaches with dark tinted windows that ferried the athletes back and forth. On the day of any big race, those buses are tough places, crowded with all kinds of people who just want to be alone. The big-shouldered sprinters are the worst. You don't want to be anywhere near them in the last hours. For them it's going to be over in ten seconds, good or bad, so they don't have room to negotiate. You've seen them – some of those hundred-metre guys are built up like superheroes or like those stone statues that are supposed to represent the perfect human form, but when the race gets close, every one of them is scared. As Burner and I squeezed our way down the aisle, we passed this big black guy sitting by himself, completely cut off from everything else. He had dark glasses on and big headphones so that nothing could get in or out and he just kept rocking back and forth, slow and silent and always on the beat so you could almost see the music he was listening to. He looked like one of those oriental monks, swaying and praying and perfectly out of it.

Burner was at the jumpy stage now and he was nearly shaking because we were on our way and it seemed like things had already started. We dumped ourselves into an unoccupied row and right away he started drumming his hands on the seat in front of us.

"I am feeling it, feeling it," he said, almost singing, and he had this big goofy grin on his face. It was impossible for him to be still even for a second and he kept drumming along on the seat, hands blurring.

"It's the big one today, boys," he shouted, revving it up.

"Got to bring everything you got." Again, way too loud.

"No tomorrow."

The clichés dribbled out of him, but this wasn't the place for it. There were too many other people around and they all had their own things to take care of. After about a minute, the tall, long-haired javelin guy who'd been sitting in front of us got up and turned around like an angry bear up on his hind legs.

"You touch this chair again," he said, and he put his finger directly on the spot where Burner had been banging away on the back of his head.

"You touch this chair again, and I swear to God, I will twist that skinny piece of shit neck right off your skinny piece of shit body."

You could tell this guy wasn't one of those macho, body builder, roid-raging throwers. He just wanted his quiet and needed his time like everybody else. You wouldn't know it by looking at them, but most of the throwers are like that, quiet and turned in. They try to make it look easy and some of them can spin a discus on their pinky finger like it's as light as a basketball, but if you watch you see they never let it go. Some of the others just sit there, rolling the shot from hand to hand, getting the feel for its heaviness as it thuds down into their chalky palms. Those guys are faster and smarter than you think. I heard someone say that all the best throwing performances come from guys with good feet and good heads. I bet the bear in front was one of the good ones. Burner couldn't retreat fast enough.

"I didn't think, man," he sort of stammered.

"I didn't know you were there. Sorry. Sorry."

I looked the bear right in the eye, just like you're supposed to, and I tried to show him that I sympathized and understood. I said "Nerves" as if that single word could explain everything about Burner.

The guy nodded and he said he knew all about that, but come on. He wasn't happy, but eventually he settled back down, sort of deflating back into his seat.

When it was over, Burner gave me this wide-eyed look of relief and pretended to wipe the sweat off his forehead and fling it to the side. Then he rested his head against the window and just watched the traffic going by.

I looked over at him and thought about all the buses we'd been on together. Almost since the early days as juniors, he'd been on every trip I had ever taken. At first, it was only short hops up to London and back or maybe Toronto, but after a while, as we kept at it and got better and better, we eventually hit the bigger circuits. Now we were only home four or five weekends a year and the rest of the time we were exactly like this, squished up against each other on a bus or on a plane, trying to sleep sitting up or trying to read our books under those little circular lights in the ceiling and always waiting for the next fast-food stop or bathroom break.

I used to think that a bus full of track people on their way to a meet was like one of those old fashioned circus trains, the kind that used to roll into a small town carrying the big top tent and pulling a bunch of different crazy looking cars, each one painted with curly red and gold swirls. You know the one I mean? In the Fisher-Price version of that train, every animal gets his own car and the necks of the giraffes stick out through a hole in the roof. All the freak show people live in that train: the strongman with his curly moustache and Tarzan outfit; the little-girl contortionist who can roll herself into a perfect circle; the guy who can take anybody's punch and never get hurt. I used to think that's what we were like, the track people. Each of us had one of those strange bodies designed to do only one thing. The lunatic high jumpers who talked to themselves could leap over their own heads and if you gave the pole vaulters a good, strong stick, they could put themselves through a third story window. The long jumpers could leap over a mid-sized station wagon and the shot putters could bench press it. Even the fragile looking, super-thin girls with their hair tied back in harmless looking ponytails. Those distance girls might be iron deficient and anorexic and maybe none of them have had a regular period in years, but they could all run a hundred and twenty miles in a week, almost a marathon a day. Those girls had pain thresholds that hadn't been discovered yet and if they tried they could slow their heart rates down so far you'd actually have to wait between the beats. We all had our special skills, our fascinating powers and we just barnstormed from city to city, performing them again and again in front of different people. Back when Burner and I started with this, every trip seemed like it was part of the tour, part of this bigger adventure, but I wasn't sure anymore. Sometimes I thought it might be better to be able to eat fire, or swallow a sword or hang upside down on the trapeze and catch my cousin as he flung himself through the air.

The hydraulic door hissed open when we got to the stadium and everybody bounced off and split-up into their natural groups. Burner and I blended in with a bunch of distance people we knew from other clubs and we checked the schedule to see if everything was running on time. The air was perfectly still and the temperature was right where we wanted it, just inching its way over toward cool. Burner breathed it in deeply through his nose and I caught the way he smiled his small, secret smile.

"You're going to have a good one today," I told him. Sometimes you can just recognize it in other people.

"Wait and see," he said. "I guess we'll find out soon enough."

That's what it's like when you taper down your training in the right way. There's just this weird feeling you get when you're finally ready to race. It's like you can barely keep your own body under control. In the beginning, when you're pounding through those early weeks of training and building up your base, you can never get away from the ache of being so deep-down tired and you feel like you're slowly breaking down, right to the core of your last, smashed cell. Eventually though, time passes and you get used to it. Everything balances out and you can kind of reset yourself on this new, higher level. Then, when you get close to the competition, you cut your mileage right back almost to nothing and start sharpening up and taking lots of rest. It's the trickiest thing to do correctly but if you can lighten up at exactly the right time, then it all kind of reverses and the hurt you put in earlier comes back out as strength. All of a sudden you feel like you have more energy than you need and everything seems easier than it should be. That's where Burner was now. I could see it. You maybe get that feeling three or four times in your life, if you're lucky.

IF I EVER HAVE A KID, I think I'll let them participate in the grade-school track meets when they're little, but that's it. Before it gets too serious, I'll move them over to something else like soccer, or basketball, or table tennis. Something with a team or something where you can put the blame on your equipment if it all goes wrong. But when my child is still little, I'm definitely going to push for the grade-school track meet because it never gets better than that. In the grade-school track meet, you give the kids one of those lumpy polyester uniforms and they turn all excited. They get the day off school and they get to cheer for their friends and maybe they get picked to be one of the four that runs the shiny baton all the way around the circle without dropping it. At the grade-school track meet, they give out ribbons that go all the way down to the "participant" level and if you do well, they read your name over the announcements at school so everybody will know about it. You get to pull on a borrowed pair of spikes and go pounding down that long runway before you jump into the sand. It's always hot and sunny and maybe your parents let you buy a drumstick or one of those over-priced red-white-and-blue popsicles from the acne-scarred high-school kid who has to ride around on a solid steel bicycle with a big yellow cooler stuck on the front. Maybe the girl with the red hair is there, the girl from the other school, the girl who wins all the longer races like you do. Maybe the newspaper takes a picture, you and the red-haired girl, standing on the top step of a plywood podium, holding all your first-place ribbons in the middle of a weedy field while all the dandelions are blowing their fuzzy heads off.

That's how it should always be. The stands should always be full of parents who don't know anything – people who can't tell the difference between what is really good and what is really bad – but they're there anyway, clapping and shouting their children's names, telling them to "go" and "go" and "go." You see why it's so nice. The lanes are crowded with kids clunking their way home to the finish line and trying so hard. They go sailing way over the high jump bar – it looks so easy – and they come down on the other side, rolling softly into those big, blue fluffy mats. It's sunny and everybody's laughing and everything is still new.

All that disappears when you get serious. At the very top end – and, when you come down to it, Burner and I were still far from the *real* top end – it's completely different. Everything starts to matter too much and there are too many things that can go wrong and everybody knows the difference between what is really good and what is really bad. It comes back to the numbers. At the top end, we count it all up and measure it out and then we print the results so everybody can see. The guys I raced against were the mathematical totals of what they had done so far. That was it. Nobody cared about your goal or about what you planned to do in the future. It might take two full years of training to drop a single second or just a couple tenths off your personal best but you couldn't complain. We were all in the same boat. For us, every little bit less was a little bit more.

Really, it's the opposite of healthy. People will do anything to make those numbers go down. Some of them gobble big spoonfuls of straight baking soda before a race even though they know it gives you this brutal, bloody diarrhea an hour later. That's nothing. It's even legal. They can't ban you for baking soda, but I know guys who cross over, guys juiced up on EPO and guys who just disappear for a year and then come back like superstars. They say they've been training at altitude on some mountain in Utah, but everybody knows they've been through the lab, getting their transfusions, and playing around with their red blood cell count. Burner and I never did that, but we used to go to this vet, a guy who worked on the race horses out at the track. If you came at night and brought him straight cash he'd give you a bottle of DMSO and a couple of these giant horse pills that you were supposed to chop up into little chunks. It sounds bad, but this was all perfectly legal too. His stuff was nothing more than super-powerful aspirin delivered in massive doses. We'd go see him and he'd say "Now you're going to have a big dinner and a full stomach before you touch this stuff, right?" and we'd lie and he'd give us what we wanted. As if he couldn't tell that none of us ever ate a full meal. I used to pop anti-inflammatories like they were candy love hearts, going through a handful of Naproxen every day.

Even the dangerous cortisone injections in those big needles, the ones they fire right into that band of tough connective tissue at the bottom of your foot, I've had those. They say you're only supposed to take three of those in your whole life – that's all a regular person can handle – but the year before the trials, I got six in five months. I just kept going to different doctors, in different crowded clinics, guys who didn't know where I'd been two weeks earlier. It was the same thing every time. They'd go through their whole spiel again, and I'd pretend to pay close attention as they explained it all out.

"You can only get three of these," they'd say, "just three, you understand?"

I'd look and nod my head seriously and sometimes I'd even write the number down for them, a big loopy three on one of their little pads and I'd underline it. Then I'd hop right up onto their tissue covered table, rip off my sock, stick out my fucked-up foot, and brace myself for number 4 or number 5 or whatever came next.

It always got bad before the biggest competitions – like this one, or before the Olympic trials or if there was a big trip to China on the line or carding money. You'd get stuck with this feeling like when you're blowing up a balloon and you know you're almost at the limit and you're not sure if you should give it that little extra puff because there might still be room for a last bit of air, or it all might just explode in your face.

BURNER AND I started our warm-up jog about an hour before the race was scheduled to go. It took me a while to get started and for those first few minutes, I hobbled along doing the old-man shuffle until my body came back to me and my

Achilles remembered what it was supposed to do. Burner was smooth right from the beginning. While I jerked up and down, fighting against the parts of myself that didn't want to do this anymore, he kind of hovered beside me flat and easy. We were like two people at the airport. He floated and seemed to move along without any effort – like one of those well-pressed, put-together guys who zooms past on the moving sidewalk – and I was like the slob with too many carry-on bags, huffing and puffing and dropping things, hauling all this extra stuff and just hoping to find the right gate. Even my breathing was heavier than it should have been.

We made a big loop out and around the stadium, winding our way up and down the quiet little side streets, past houses full of people who couldn't care less about what was happening just down the road. Burner and I had probably run thousands of miles together, but I was pretty sure these would be the last ones. I'd been thinking about it for a while, but I decided it there, during that last little warm-up jog. I think all those houses where nobody cared kind of forced themselves into my head.

"This is going to be it for me," I told him, after about fifteen minutes.

"What do you mean 'it'?"

"This is it. The last real ball-buster race for me. I think it's over. Time to get on with everything else."

It was easier than I thought it would be. All you had to do was say it. As soon as the words came out of my mouth, I felt better and calmer, but Burner didn't take it the same way.

"What?" he said and he looked at me with this kind of confused sneer.

"Come on, Mikey. What else is there for you to do? You can't be finished. You've got lots more in the tank. You can't be one of those guys who gives it up and sits on the couch for a year eating chips and dip. You'll never be the guy in the fun run, the guy with a walkman, the loser who wants to win his age-group. You can't just turn it off like that."

I felt bad for springing this on him at such a bad time. It hadn't been part of my big plan, but it's hard to hide it when something that used to be important suddenly isn't important anymore. I felt like I was kind of abandoning him, dumping him out there in the middle of those empty houses and it was difficult and sad and correct all at the same time. Like when my mother and father finally broke up: difficult and sad, yes, but correct too, the right thing to do. Burner should have seen this coming from me. He could read the results sheets as well as I could and he knew where my name fit in.

"I've gone as far as I can," I told him. "You know you can't do this if you don't have the feel for it."

"Come on," he said, "you're kidding me."

He reached over without breaking stride and gave me a little shot in the arm like he was trying to wake me up and bring me back to the real world.

"Give your head a shake," he said. "Think about next year. You'll heal up and be back good as new."

We turned the corner and I could see the stadium coming back to us, getting bigger all the time. The stiffness was gone from my legs and I was rolling now, back to my old self, purring along. I felt fine, better than I had in months. The taper was giving something back to me too. But I was sure about this.

"Sorry, buddy," I kidded him. "You're going to have to find somebody else to kick down in the last hundred."

"Stop it," Burner said. He was looking at me hard. His lips pressed together and his mouth made a tight straight line across the middle of his face.

"Seriously. Stop it. You can't quit now. You and I do this together. That's our deal."

"No," I said, "it's not." I thought he already knew about this part of it.

"We have never done this together. It's one of those things that can't be done together. In the end we have to be by ourselves."

I didn't want it to sound as bad as it did.

"Think about it," I was smiling now, trying to show him that everything would be fine.

"Think about it. When you come around that turn today, you'll be alone and when you head down the stretch by yourself you are going to surprise a lot of people."

"Fuck you, Mikey," he said. "I don't need a cheerleader."

His face was a little flush and he turned on me quickly.

"You're just covering your own ass. In about twenty minutes, I'm going to rip you apart and you can't stand it. You can't stand to lose to me and now you're making excuses. Fuck you and your retirement party."

I wanted to laugh if off and make it slide away, but before I could even get to him, before I could say anything, he took off. Burner put his head down and shifted gears. In ten seconds, he had pulled away and opened up a gap that couldn't be closed. I had to save everything I had left and I couldn't go chasing after him so I let him go. It was just jitters, just nerves. That's what I told myself. After it was over, everything would be fine again.

When we got back to the field we split for good. He grabbed his spikes and his bag and went under the bleachers by himself. The last fifteen minutes is the most important. You want everything to feel easy. I put him out of my mind and lay on my back for a while, feeling the air coming in and going out of my body. I pulled my knees up close to my chest and wrapped my arms around my legs. I held it all in like that for about fifteen seconds before letting everything go as slowly as possible. I rolled over on my stomach and did a few easy push-ups and when I got back on my feet, I put my hands flat against the wall and tried to get my calves and my goddamn Achilles to go out as far as they could. I didn't want to push it because you can only take as much as your body can give you on the day. I took off my socks and put on the ugly fluorescent spikes I'd been wearing all season. They were another Adidas freebee, and I was expected to wear them, but I didn't like them much. It had taken months to break them in and the red blood stains were still there around the toe and heel from all the broken blisters I had to go through before my feet finally hardened up in the right places.

When the announcer's voice called us out, I took off my sweats and did a couple short sprints down the back stretch, trying to keep it all quick and smooth and under control. All the rest of the guys were there too and we did our usual nervous hellos and our cautious smiles as we passed one another. When they called us to the line, I came up behind Burner and put my hand on his back, just kind of gently, so he'd know I was there.

"Have a good one, buddy, you little psycho," I said and I smiled at him. The officials made us stand there, side by side, each of us in our pre-selected spot along the curved white start line while the announcer read out our names and listed all our best times and our biggest wins. He said this was shaping up to be one of the best 1,500 metre finals of the last decade. When the voice got to my name, he said I had the fastest personal best in this group and he named all the different times I'd made the national team. He said Burner was always dangerous and that he had put together a great season and was rounding into top form at the right time. Then the rest of them each got their turns and their compliments, Marcotte and Graham and Bourque and the others.

Burner stood still through all of this and didn't even acknowledge his own name. Instead, he closed his eyes and made this big production out of rolling his head all the way around in a big circle. He went very slowly – first down, with his chin touching his chest, and then way over to the side and then straight up and back again. I could hear the bones in his neck crackling as he made the loop. He kept his mouth wide open and when he looked up, it seemed almost like he was waiting to catch a snowflake or a raindrop on his tongue. They called us to our marks and we crouched down, bending our knees just a bit and holding our arms away from our bodies. When they fired the gun, you could see the smoke before you heard the bang.

The announcer's voice took over after that and he described everything that happened to us. We were bunched up around the first turn so I made a little move and went into second place, just trying to stay out of trouble. Even as it was happening, the voice said "There goes Michael Campbell, moving into second place, staying out of trouble." It was like being inside and outside of yourself at the same time. I kept bumping back and forth with Marcotte and Bourque, trying to settle myself down and find a clear place on the outside of lane one. All the time the big voice kept going, describing how we looked and calling out the splits and telling the crowd what kind of pace we were on and our projected finishing times. I couldn't see Burner, but I knew he was close by because I heard the voice say something like "Jamie Burns is safely tucked in at fifth or sixth place." I remember this only because the announcer used Burner's real name and it sounded so strange to me.

The pace was fine, not really too slow or too fast, and after a lap and a half there were still lots of people close enough to the lead and feeling good. The problem with feeling good in a 1,500 is that you know it can't last and that eventually, sometime in the next ninety seconds, everything you have left has got to come draining out of you, either in a great explosive rush at the end or some painful slow trickle. The kickers would've been happy to let it go slow and leave it all to some blazing last one-fifty, but the rest of us didn't want that to happen. As we went through 800, most of the serious guys were looking around, waiting and watching to see who would make the first move. After about thirty seconds, Dawson decided it would have to be him. He threw in this big surge coming off the turn and broke the whole thing open, dividing the race up between those who could go with him and those who could not.

The voice said, "Eric Dawson is heading for home early."

Graham and Bourque and I hooked up a couple steps back and it felt like we were breaking free of the others. I never turn around when I race and everybody knows it's not a good idea to look back, but I was sure Burner must have been close by. Even then it was clear that Dawson didn't have a chance. He'd given it a pretty fierce try and the rest of us probably owed him something for being brave enough to go, but he didn't have enough left and I could see he was starting to break down.

People in the crowd always wonder why the guy with the lead heading into the last lap almost never wins. They wonder why he can't hold on and why he can't look as good as he did just a minute earlier when he came flying by. Some people believe that myth about Roger Bannister and John Landy back when they ran the Miracle Mile in Vancouver in 1954. That was probably the only time in history when the whole world actually cared about two guys who could run a mile in under four minutes. Bannister was the first to do it, everybody knows that, but by the time they met in Vancouver, Landy had gone even faster. He was the new world record holder and most people were betting on him to win. You can look it up if you want. The Miracle Mile was pure craziness, the Tyson/Holyfield of its time. Every country sent their reporters to cover the story and more than a hundred million people listened to the call on the radio. It was the first time CBC Television ever broadcasted live from the west coast. If you go to Vancouver today, the famous statue is still there, the one where Landy is looking over his left shoulder as Bannister comes by him on the right. The press and people who don't know anything always say that if Landy had looked the other way – if only he'd looked to the right – he would have seen Bannister coming and he never would have let him go by. They call it the phantom pass, as if Landy was just a victim of bad luck and bad timing. As if Bannister was like some ghost, slipping past unseen.

That's the story they tell, but it's not true. If you ever watch a tape of that race you'll see that poor Landy is dead before he even starts the last lap. It's one of those things you recognize if you've been through it yourself. When a guy is done, he's just done and no amount of fighting can save him. The exercise physiology people will explain that it's all about lactic acid fermentation and how when you push beyond your limit your legs run out of oxygen and the tissue starts to fill up with this burning liquid waste. We called it "rigging," short for rigor mortis. When your body started to constrict, to tighten up involuntarily, first in your arms and your calves and then your quads and your hamstrings and your brain – when parts of you gave out like that, dying right underneath you at exactly the moment you needed something more – we called that rigging. Dawson was dying in front of us that day and we could see it in every broken down step he took. Look back at the grainy black and white video of the Miracle Mile. You'll see it. Landy wasn't taken by surprise. He knew exactly where Bannister was coming from – he just couldn't do anything to stop it. For that whole last lap Bannister is right behind, tall and gangly and awkward and just waiting, deciding when to go. When Landy looked to his left – in that moment they made into a statue – he wasn't trying to hold on for the win. That possibility was gone and he knew it. People forget that Richard Ferguson, a Canadian, finished third in the Miracle Mile. He's the important missing character, the one who didn't make it into the statue. Ferguson was the threat coming up from behind; he was the guy Landy feared. It's always like that. The most interesting stories in most races don't have anything to do with winning.

DAWSON WAS ALMOST SHAKING when we came by him. The last lap was going to be a death march for him. Graham and Bourque and I went past in a single step and there was nothing left in Dawson to go with us.

The voice said, "Graham, Bourque, Campbell. It will be decided by these three."

I couldn't believe I was still in it and feeling okay. Graham looked like he was getting ready to drop the hammer and put an end to this, but as we headed down the final back stretch Bourque seemed a little wobbly and for about five seconds, I thought I had a real shot at bringing him down and getting myself in there for second and a spot on the team. I was just about to release my own kick, trying to gauge how much I had left and deciding how I could fit it into that last 250 metres. I got up on my toes and was getting ready to charge when I felt this hand reach out and touch the middle of my back, kind of gently, just a tap so I'd know he was there. I looked to my right and Burner came roaring by with his tongue hanging out and that enraged look in his eyes.

The voice said "Look at that. Burns is making a very strong move."

I UNDERSTAND THAT sometimes people get their priorities mixed-up. And I know that when you give yourself over completely to just one thing, you can lose perspective on the rest of the world. That's a feeling I know. I think it's what happens to those old ladies who donate their life savings to corrupt televangelists or to those pilgrims in the Philippines who compete for the honour of being nailed, actually hammered, to a cross for their Easter celebrations. We have to scrounge for meaning wherever we can find it and there's no way to separate our faith from our desperation. You see it everywhere. Football hooligans, scholars of Renaissance poetry, fans of heavy metal music, car buffs, sexual perverts, collectors of all kinds, extreme bungee jumpers, lonely physicists, long distance runners and tightly wound suburban housewives who want to make sure they entertain in just the right way. All of us. We can only value what we yearn for and it really does not matter what others think.

This is why I cannot expect you to understand that when Jamie Burns came past me and started up that now infamous kick which won him the national title in the 1,500 metres – his wild, chased-by-the-train-sprint that carried him around me, past Bourque and all the way up to Graham – I cannot expect you to understand that when this happened, I was caught up, caught up for the first and only time in my life, in one of those pure ecstatic surges that I believed only religious people ever experienced. Even as it unfolded in front of me and I watched Graham hopelessly trying to hold him off, I knew I had never wanted anything more than this, just to see Burner come up even and then edge his way forward in those last few steps and come sailing across the line with both his hands in the air. I did not care that this was such a small thing or that it could be shared with so few. I knew only that this event, this little victory mattered to me in some serious way that was probably impossible to communicate. I didn't pray for it to happen because there would be nobody to receive a prayer like that. But I did wish for it and even the wish told me something I had never known about myself before. We are what we want most and there are no miracles without desire. That's why a mom can lift a car off her child after the accident and a guy can survive a plane crash and live in the woods for a week drinking only the sweat wrung from his socks. That's how Burner won that race, by miraculous desperation.

If you are not the person who wins, then the finish line of a 1,500 can be a crowded place. There are bodies collapsing and legs giving out and people wandering around with dazed and exhausted looks on their faces. Burner's kick caught everybody by surprise. Even the announcer lost control of the story. For the last fifty meters he just kept shouting "Will you look at that. Look. It's Burns at the end. Look."

I'd been so busy watching that nothing changed for me. I ended up exactly where I was before and never got past Bourque. I finished fourth, the worst place to be, but it was still more than I expected. People from the paper were taking pictures as I walked over to Burner. When he turned around we both just started laughing and shaking our heads.

"You bastard," I said and I pounded both my fists against his shoulders.

"Where did that come from? How in the hell . . ."

"No idea," he said. "I thought I was out of it, but I decided to go in the end and everything else just happened."

Other people, strangers I had never seen before, were coming around slapping him on the back and giving their congratulations. The whole place was still kind of quivering because no one had ever seen a guy come back from being that far down. Every eye was on Burner and everyone was talking about that last stretch and trying to find a place for it in their own personal histories.

One of the drug officials came over and took Burner away to go pee in his cup and prove that everything was natural. As he was being led off, he turned back and told me to wait for him.

"You're going to be busy," I said. "Forget it."

"Just wait," he said.

For those next fifteen minutes I was kind of stuck between two different versions of my self. I wandered back over to my bag and started to get dressed again. I looked around the track and it seemed like this big chunk of my past was kind of crystallizing behind me and freezing into permanence. Whatever the next thing would be was still way ahead, indistinct and foggy and I had no idea what it would look like. I pulled off those ugly spikes and in a mock-dramatic moment I tossed them into a garbage can and I just stood there for a while feeling the cool grass on my bare feet.

Burner came jogging back from his test soon after that, but every step he took there was somebody else there shaking his hand and patting the top of his bald head. All around him people were smiling and a couple of younger kids asked for his autograph and wanted to get their pictures taken with him. Burner drank it in like one of those actors standing on the red carpet before the Oscars begin and even though it took him a while to make it across the track, he kept looking up at me every couple seconds, letting me know that I was still the final destination and our planned warm-down was still going to take place.

When he finally made it over he had this ridiculously huge grin on his face and he kind of shrugged his shoulders.

"What can you do?" he said. "It's all crazy."

"They get your pee?" I asked. "Everything okay in that department?"

"No problem," he said.

He pulled on a dry T-shirt and his own pair of high-tech sweatpants and said he was ready to go.

When we made it out of the stadium everything quieted down very quickly. The announcer's voice had moved on to the final of the women's 400 hurdles and we could just barely hear him as we turned away and went backwards along the same streets we had run earlier. Whenever you do that – go back along the same course, but in the opposite direction – it's strange how some scenes are so familiar and others look so completely different you wonder how you missed them the first time around. It's just the change in perspective, but sometimes, especially when you're in a foreign city, you can get yourself pretty disoriented and lost. Then you have to slow down and look around and try and locate a recognizable landmark before you can be sure you're on the right track.

Burner and I fell into a nice rhythm right away and our feet clipped along almost in unison. We went back past all those houses where nobody cared and it felt fine and comfortable. Our breathing was the only conversation and it said that we were both relaxed and taking it easy. Some of the neighbourhood kids were still out shooting baskets in their driveways and practicing tricks with their skateboards.

We just floated down those anonymous sidewalks and carved our way though the maze of minivans and garbage cans. We made a turn and were just about to head back to the stadium when a bunch of kids came streaking past us on their bikes. There were four or five of them, a couple boys and a couple girls, probably between the ages of seven and nine. Real kids, not yet teenagers. One of the boys almost hit us as he went by and another one kept trying to jump his BMX up and down over the driveway cut-outs of the curb. There was a girl on a *My Little Pony* bike. She had multi-coloured beads on all her spokes and red and white streamers trailing back from her handlebars. Her hair was wispy and blonde. As she came by, she turned around and yelled "I'm faster than you are." She sort of sang it in a mean, bratty way, using the same up-and-down teasing music that accompanies every "nah, nah, nah, nah, nah."

"You can't catch me," she said and she stuck her tongue out and pedalled harder. Her pink shoes swivelled around in circles.

One of the boys, a kid wearing a tough-looking camouflage T-shirt, zipped around us and swerved in tight to cut me off. As he pulled away, he shot us the finger and said "Nice tights, loser."

I glanced over at Burner and said "Let it go," but it was too late. His face was tightening up and that angry stare was coming back into his eyes. He wasn't looking at me.

"Hey," he yelled and you could feel the edges hardening around that one little syllable. He pulled ahead of me and started tracking them down. I was caught unprepared and a step behind and I couldn't figure out how we had managed to arrive at this point. Burner was charging again and the kids were running. They didn't know. There was no way on earth they could have known. The little girl was pedalling as fast as she could and there was this strange, high-pitched, wheezing sound coming out of her, but there was nothing she could do. Burner had already closed the gap and his hand was already there, reaching out for the thin strands of her hair. It all disintegrated after that. He must have been a foot taller than the oldest one.

Wonder About Parents

Lice. The third week. Head checks in the morning and head checks at night after the baths. You need to go slowly. A separate bath for every person. New water. Fresh pillow cases every night. New sheets. New blankets. The washing machine is going to die. Hats and T-shirts and hooded sweatshirts. Brushes and combs and hair elastics. Water boiling in the kettle. Everything that touches us needs to be scalded.

What to look for. The eggs, nits, stuck to the shaft, close to the scalp. Dark if they're fresh, translucent if they've already hatched. A seven-day gestation cycle. The nymphs, freshly born, almost impossible to spot without experience. You learn to see. A dot that shouldn't be there, smaller than a comma or a freckle, moving, but not mature enough to reproduce. Seven more days to reach full growth. The adults are grey and black, size of a poppy seed. They hate the light and run from it, down the part in a child's hair. Wingless, flightless, they crawl from head to head. One mature louse can lay ten eggs a day, one hundred fifty eggs in a lifetime. Around the ears, the base of the neck, the crown: these are the warmest spots on the human skull. Kids scratched raw. Bleeding sometimes.

The shampoo is not so bad – more flower than chemical – but it tingles and has to stay on the head for ten minutes to work. The pharmacist will put it in a discreet paper bag and whisper to you about side-effects. Asthmatics should seek alternative treatment. Between application and rinsing, we walk around wearing matching towels and shower caps. Same treatment for everybody, even the two-year-old.

Don't touch. Don't rub your eyes.

Bag hat, she says, scrunching it with her fingers. Funny bag hat.

Ten minutes on each head. Enough time for the killing ingredient to soak all the way through. De-lousing. Then rinse. Naked kids, braced between our legs, standing under the shower. Facecloths over their eyes and mouths. Don't swallow any of this water. Spit it out. Spit right now. A scar on our daughter's stomach from before. We go through with a fine-toothed comb. It is made of metal, comes in a plastic sleeve with the shampoo. Every inch of every head every night. The box says repeat application after seven days. Repeat again if infestation persists. It has been three weeks. Thought we were finished and clear. Then, today, a perfect specimen, a text book example, crawling out of our daughter's bangs.

Treats for everyone who is good. For everyone who can stay still, who doesn't complain or scratch or talk about it. A secret. Only for the people who live in this house.

Chicken bugs, chicken bugs, says the youngest. Bugs that lay eggs on your head.

Notes sent out on blue paper. The school is overrun. Public health. A new look for the oldest. Tight braids woven close to her head. Stare at other kids coming off the bus. Which one of you is the source of this? Wonder about parents. The fine lines. Different levels of commitment. Who is lazy and who is not? Dirty or clean. It makes no difference. Together no matter how you feel about it. All of us moving through at the same time. Shared threats. Cross-contamination. One passed hat, two kids leaning over the same desk. Good Lego.

A colouring book. Clay. Work too close and the whole cycle starts again.

WE DO BATH and we do pyjamas and we do story. The Magic School Bus becomes a lizard, then a moth. Ms. Frizzle. A lesson about camouflage. How to hide in plain sight. Tucking in. Kisses and hugs. Settling down. Noise. Whispers and rustling at first, then steady breathing in the rooms. Quiet. Nine o'clock.

I sit on the couch. Nothing for three minutes. Strange thick silence in the house. Water running in the pipes. The last two hours of a day. Aftermath.

She comes down, still wet from the shower. T-shirt and underwear.

Okay, she says, I'll do you and you do me.

My head in her lap. Gooseneck desk lamp pulled down close. Bulb warm on the base of my neck. Our dishwasher hums. She works the metal comb through my hair. Rolls my skull from side to side, up and down, front to back. Ten minutes. Taps her fingers on my temple.

All done, she says. Nothing new. Nothing I can see.

My mouth on the elastic of her underwear. The smell of lotion. Soap.

We switch. Her face in my crotch.

I wouldn't get any ideas if I were you, Romeo.

Fold the rows of her hair with a skewer from the shish kebab set. Need to follow straight lines. Keep everything systematic. Front to back, side to side, up and down. It takes half an hour with long hair. She falls almost asleep. I pull an egg down the whole length of the shaft. Find one living insect, mature. Pluck it from her skin and watch it wriggle on my middle finger. Bring my thumb down hard. All the strength I can muster. The pressure between two points, crushing. I separate my fingers. The legs are stilled. Its body rests in a circle of her blood. Red seeps into my fingerprint. Parasite. Life sucked from our lives.

My hand on her cheek.

All done.

She comes back. Sleepy drool. The open slot of my Christmas boxers. Wetness around Rudolph the Red Nosed Reindeer.

Are we good? she says.

Yeah. Only one live one.

I guess that's progress.

Can't go on forever.

No.

She touches her fingertips to her forehead and runs them from the hairline over her eyelids and down to her cheeks.

Tired.

I know.

I'm going to go up now. Don't you stay too long. Big day tomorrow.

Yes.

Night.

It's going to be okay.

I know.

Good night.

*

If you blow up an adult louse three hundred times, you can see its claws. Black and white shots in all the brochures and pamphlets. Textured stills taken with a good camera and a microscope. The things I have learned in the last three weeks. Websites. A book from the library: *Rats, Lice, and History* by Hans Zinsser, written in 1934. What he tells me: "As far as we can ascertain, since man has existed, the louse has been his inseparable companion." Aristotle believed they came from nothing, that lice were the only creatures in life that 'generated spontaneously.' Part of our bodies, he thought, proceeding directly from us. Born out of human sweat. He couldn't get close enough. Couldn't imagine their cycle. But look now. Obvious when you magnify. Females and their eggs. Sticky, water resistant sacs glued to a thread. Three pairs of pinchers for each adult. Tight and knife sharp. Worse than a lobster. Look at the stills. Each of the six legs wrapped around a single strand of hair. Or digging into the scalp. They drink your blood. Found one in a 5,000-year-old Egyptian tomb. Still there. Holding onto the carefully braided hair of a mummified little girl.

*

The present tense. Everything happens here. A guy banging on the front door of the university house she shares with four other girls. Late on a Friday night. My first time in this place. One of her roommates moaning in the next room. Our beds less than a foot apart, separated by drywall and air. Give it to me, the girl on the other side says. Coos up high like a bird. Give it to me.

We are her unintended audience. Quiet. Rolled eyes and suppressed giggles. Oh, the ecstasy, she whispers to me. Back of her hand on her forehead. Half-open mouth. The ecstasy. We laugh. Move in silence.

The knocking comes loud and fast. Shakes us up. Somebody with a purpose in the middle of the night. He screams her name. Hammers on the aluminum door frame. Her name first, then the strike. Knuckles on the windows. Glass rattling near its breaking point. Hear the ping. We are nineteen years old. Four or five in the morning. What was his name? The guy banging on the windows that night? The guy calling for you?

He howls for five minutes. Gets tired. Goes away. We think he's played out, but no.

I know you're in there.

Banging. Hard cracking in his voice.

I'm sorry, he says. I just want to talk. I screwed it up. I know. I'm sorry.

I know you're there.

Two seconds of nothing, then he turns.

I swear to fucking God.

Hard strike. Something rattles loose in the frame.

If there's anybody else in there with you.

Bang.

His shoulder and a running start. Slamming himself against the door. Feel the give in the walls. Deep tremor moving through the house.

I'm coming in. I told you I'm sorry. There better not be anybody there.

The roommate shouts, I'm going to call the cops.

I move to get up, push the covers away. I am taller than I am now.

I'll talk to him, I say. He needs to move on before the police show up and it gets ugly.

Pants and shoes. Fumbling for a shirt. Her hand on my arm pulling me back down. A shushing finger. Something extra, left over from another episode.

Stay, she whispers.

Come on. He's just a drunk. He'll move along.

She shakes her head.

What?

Nothing. Just stay and be quiet. He'll give up.

Origins. A pretty girl in a bar. Notice her Clash T-shirt. Combat Rock. Probably second-hand. Thin and worn out. Almost see through. The way it follows her body. We walk out of the city snow and into the same place at the same time. That is it. Strangers. Open mic night at *The Bridge*. Cold swirl of white moving in the air behind us. See it again whenever the door is opened. Unwind our scarves. Pitchers of draft. Nothing to each other. Small talk. What is your middle name? Do you have any brothers or sisters? Where exactly do you come from? Band flyers taped to the walls in her room. A beaded curtain and candles. Starting off. How to do this the right way. Then the noise. A guy banging at the door. He is the entire past. The only person I have ever met who knows who you are.

Come back, she says. Rubs her hand on the sheet.

I take off my pants. Move under the covers. She pulls them up over our heads. Our breathing, hot in the tent. Dark.

She lifts her hand under the blanket. Opens a little space for us. My eyes adjust. See her outline coming out of the black. We are hooking up. That is what it's called.

My grandmother made this blanket, she says, running her finger down the seam. She quilts. Can make one of these out of the scraps in the rag bin. Lived in the same farm house all her life.

Oh yeah? Where about?

In the county. Albuna. Know where that is?

The boy outside goes quiet. Never see his face. We sleep. Futon mattress on the floor. Broken clock radio blinking: 12:00, 12:00, 12:00. A night when nothing happens.

*

Since the beginning of time, Zinsser says. Every culture that has ever lived, everywhere in the world. Exclusively human. They cannot jump the species barrier or survive on other mammals. Pygmies and the medieval English embraced their medicinal properties. Made soup out of lice. Ate them sun-dried or roasted. The cure for jaundice, for eczema, for impotence. Young girls in Siberia collected their parasites and tossed them at potential suitors like confetti. A demonstration of fertility, proof of a warm body in a cold climate. Aztec peasants filled whole sacks, an entire village's worth. Offered them up at the temple. What you have when you have nothing. The Chinese thought lice could predict the sex of unborn children. Something about the way it crawls down your stomach. And the Swedes. The Swedes at election time made all the mayoral candidates rest their beards on the kitchen table. Then they released one adult female and watched her climb into the chin of their leader for the next year. That is how you make a decision.

*

Winter. We live in Montreal. Blow-dried plastic on the windows. Three pairs of socks. The washing machine freezes solid in the back room. Our clothes encased in a block of ice. First Christmas with a baby. She is four months old and sick. Fever for two days. Don't know what to do. Thermometer under her arm. Hold her down and wait for the beep. One hundred and two. One hundred and three. Something in her body not working right. Wrap her tight. Swaddle her the way they teach in the books. *What to Expect When You're Expecting.* Not good enough. She shakes free. Sleeps in fits. Rolls hard against the crib railings. Reaches out with her arms. Opens and closes her small fists. Infant with a nightmare. Watch it pass through, but cannot make it go away. She dreams but can't talk. The brain of a four--month-old. Try to imagine her seeing. The vague bad thing in her mind. How big? What does it look like tonight?

The drive home is ten hours in good conditions. Ten hours in the summer.

Let's stay here, she says. Just the three of us. Christmas with ourselves. We need to start somewhere. The baby's sick and nobody is sleeping right. They'll understand.

You know we have to go, I say. You know that. Other people have plans. It's been locked in for months. Christmas and the new baby. Everybody wants to see the baby.

She points at our kid.

Look at her, she says. She's sick. Nobody wants to see a sick baby. Why can't we stay just ourselves? This is it now. Can't belong to two sets of people at the same time.

You know we have to go.

She shakes her head.

Tell me you know it's going to suck. Tell me you know it's going to suck. Tell me you understand that.

It's going to suck. I'm sorry.

Okay then. Thank you. Settled. I just need to know that you know.

BAD PACKING. The folding playpen. Extra blankets. Cooler for breast milk. All the baby's gear. Three suitcases. Shovel the car out of its spot. We are weighed down and riding low.

The baby throws up after only fifteen minutes. Stuck on the Decarie with no way off. Bumper to bumper. The smell. Hot milk vomit soaking through the car seat. Blowing snow. Whiteout conditions. Everyone trying to keep their tires inside the two black lines. Ten hours of driving on a good day. Need to make time in the daylight. Everything harder when it gets dark.

A brutal diarrhea in Belleville. Green splashing over the sides of a fold-down change table in the guy's bathroom of the rest stop. Liquid shit blasts out of her diaper, runs all the way up her back to the neck. Poop in her hair. Lines of men waiting for the urinals, watching me.

Got your hands full there, buddy.

An entire outfit. White overalls and a long-sleeved shirt. Noah's Ark. Osh Kosh b'Gosh. It all snaps open at the crotch. Probably worth fifty dollars in the store, but it can't be saved. Even the socks. I go through my entire supply of wipes. Grit my teeth. Roll the whole mess into a ball and drive it into the garbage. Bring the baby back out in just her diaper and an undershirt. Pink boots pinched between my fingers. She is tucked inside my coat. Feel her wriggling in tight. Marsupial. Burrowing down against the cold.

WHAT HAPPENED? Where are her clothes?

Full-scale blowout. Had to ditch them. Completely saturated. No way to save that outfit.

But they're brand new.

Believe me: they're lost. Those are clothes she used to have. Go back.

I threw them away. They're in the garbage.

They're a present. My mother gave those to us. We'll clean them up. Go back.

No. Come on.

I'm going then.

The men's john? They're lined up twenty deep in there.

If you won't go, I'm going to go.

PULL BACK on the stainless steel chute. Dig through the paper towels. Find the ball. Water running through the tiny denim legs. Green circling down the drain. Stuff the filth into a shopping bag. New layer of stench for the car.

We squirt cherry-flavoured Tylenol into her mouth with an eyedropper. Fresh pyjamas, fresh blankets. The heater kicks in. Engine hits its regular vibration. The baby falls into a deep, drug-induced car sleep.

*

Partial list of substances people have put on their heads to kill lice: rendered dog fat, glasses of human spit, mercury, arsenic, cedar oil, garlic paste and oregano, Ching-Hao, pyrethrum, ground poppies, borax, Vaseline, honey, frankincense, vinegar, bull semen, salt and pepper, mustard, mayonnaise, wormwood, cat urine, beet juice, tobacco, lard, kerosene, gasoline, turpentine, eucalyptus, snake venom.

*

Our son in the back seat. He has a booster, sits in the middle, between the girls. We wait in line at the drive-thru.

I ask the speaker: What does a Happy Meal come with?

Pay at the first window. At the second, a lady hands us bags of food, a tray of drinks.

He holds up his hands and says, I am free, right? I am free and I live in Dark Myth.

Not paying attention.

Yes, I say. That's right. You're free. That's nice.

But his big sister shakes her head.

Not free, she says. Look at him, you big duh head.

I turn around. He is trying to make his thumb touch his pinky finger.

Not free, she says. He means three.

He is three. He is three and he lives in Dartmouth.

Oh, I say. Okay. I get that. Yes. Three and Dartmouth. That, too.

*

Line from Zinsser: "The louse – like man – has, for one reason or another, failed to develop the highly complex civilization of the bee or the ant."

*

Seething quiet in the front seat almost all the way to Toronto. Her head against the window. Half her reflection looking back. I punch the seek button. Look for reliable radio signals to carry us through. Approach the city. Buildings rise and lanes crowd. Condos overlooking the 401. Backlit windows. A single guy watching a hockey game on a big screen TV. Bag of chips in his lap. Bottle of beer. Feet up on the coffee table. He sits in the sky as we pass.

Everybody on their way. Express and collector. Keep your distance. A two-car-length minimum. Exit for the 404, Exit for the 407. Don't get trapped by the QEW. Don't go to Hamilton. My right blinker. My right blinker again. The polite wave. Adjust to the pace. Small openings where someone will let you in. Tight margins. Sweat on the steering wheel.

Her hand comes gentle on my shoulder. Fingers pressing the back of my neck.

You're doing great, she says. A single, real smile. Once we get through this section, we'll be fine.

I touch her leg. Rub my hand against her jeans. Friction and warmth. The thin bone of her kneecap. Tendons holding it in place. We are moving over asphalt. 130 kilometers per hour. A used Toyota Tercel. More than 250,000 clicks on the odometer. Thin doors. Rust. All-season tires. No air bags. Baby-On-Board sign suction-cupped to the back window.

Guelph and Cambridge. Woodstock and London. Dark snow on the windshield. We run out of washer fluid and have to refill. A bottle of bright blue-40 glugging into the reservoir. Skull and crossbones. Symbols for explosion and corrosion. A phone number for poison control.

Then the long, long hypnotizing flat. Sleepy last sections. Chatham and Tilbury. Gas stations that were shut down five years ago. See the Bridge rising, the Renaissance Center like a mirage though we are still half an hour away.

We pull in three hours late. Tired, but home. The house is lit up. Christmas tree. Everyone waiting. My adult brothers and sisters, my parents. We move around each other in the living room. What we were and what we are.

The baby makes the rounds. First grandchild. New generation. Sleeps through her introduction.

Isn't she big?

And all the hair she's got.

The little fingernails. Look at the little fingernails.

Couldn't I just eat her up?

My mother puts her hand on the baby's cheek.

She feels very hot to me. Do you think she feels hot?

Yeah. She's been sick. Pretty bad. A high fever for two or three days.

That's not good, she says to me. You need to be very, very careful with them when they're this small. Anything could have happened out there on the road.

My wife's breathing. Out hard through her nose. She slumps in a chair. Closes her eyes.

*

Lice killed thirty million people after World War I. Typhus. Jails and slums and soldiers' barracks. Fever and stiffening joints. The rash, raw coughing, fast fall into delirium. The word typhus comes from the Greek for fog. A mist settling in your brain. Poor people first, then anybody forced to live too close to anybody else. Impossible to contain. How does it spread? A mystery at first. Some see a curse or a plague. Punishment for something done wrong. Absolutely inescapable once it entered your house. The chain of events. Your sister's dementia leading to your father's fade. No small significances lost. The first moment you feel a little warmer than you did before. The first time you cough.

*

On TV. The same thing for weeks. So, so boring. A map of the world and a map of the country. Hot spots. Outbreaks. The global pandemic. Be afraid. A brand new bug. Unexpected mutation. Completely unforeseen. Only the elderly, people who lived through the Spanish Flu of 1917, will be able to fight it off. Antibodies they do not even know they have. The peak of the second wave. The approach of the third. Surgical masks and latex gloves. Vials of vaccine. Bad orders, expired shipments. The government, people say, the government. Ridiculous panic in the eyes of people who always, always panic. Protesters. Who will be saved? In what order? Teachers and firemen and front line workers. Who should get it first? Letters to the editor. A woman interviewed. She is hysterical. But I work with people, she says. I work with people. Adjuvanted and unAdjuvanted. Pregnant women and kids under five. People with underlying medical conditions. The twelve-year-old hockey player, the forty-two-year-old mountain climber. There was nothing wrong with them.

Our son says I don't want to get shot. Don't take me to the place where I get shot.

No, honey. Nobody is going to shoot you. Just a needle, a little pinch so you won't get sick. They have stickers and orange juice. You get a sticker when it's over.

A needle?

Yes, just a little pinch and that's it.

I don't want to get needled. Don't take me to the place where I get needled.

INOCULATION.

If you get up early and wait in the line, I'll bring the kids around at eight. That way they won't have to stand out in the cold for hours.

You know this is nothing, right? Mass hysteria. TV makes them do it. In two weeks, just you watch, no one will care anymore. They'll move on to the next thing. You know that, right?

Yes. All crazy. Yes. All crazy until one of them gets sick because we didn't get them a dose of free vaccine from a free clinic. Then what is it?

Okay.

So you line up and I'll bring them over at eight.

Good.

STAND IN THE DARK with the others. Young fathers with cellphones and the same idea. Teenage girls and their strollers.

Minus ten and four hours to go. Limited options. A dozen Dora the Explorers sleeping on the sidewalk. Thermoses and donuts. Reliable grandparents picking up the slack, covering the bases. Lawn chairs and blankets. Half-conscious snow-suited toddlers. We are close enough. Front of the line. The door is there and it will open at eight.

A kid completely coated in the white goop from a cinnamon roll.

My thoughts. That stuff is going to jam your zipper, my friend. No way around it. His mom is pregnant. She looks at my jacket and my boots. Takes a deep, slow drag on her cigarette.

Your wife is going to come with the kids just before they open the doors, isn't she?

Yeah, that's what we're thinking.

Thought so.

She sucks back the last heat from her cigarette. Flings the filter against the wall. Nods over to her son.

You watch him and hold my spot and I'll bring you back a coffee.

No problem.

When she returns, we drink it down quietly. Feel the warm moving through. Talk about the price of diapers. Second-hand snowsuits. Value Village. They grow so fast. Three pairs of boots last winter, I swear to God. Stupid to get anything new.

My kids pull up at ten to eight. Clean faces and warm hats. Their snow pants have their names written on the tags.

A guy from the back comes forward.

No cutting, he says. Eyes empty and tired. He wants to enforce the lining up law.

I tell him I've been holding this spot since four in the morning. The cinnamon roll mom nods her head.

My wife looks in the other direction. Raises an eyebrow at me. Shrugs. The kids are quiet. This has nothing to do with them.

But the cinnamon roll lady won't back down. Gets up in his face.

Right fucking here since right fucking four, she says. He held the places and I got the coffees. We've been here since the beginning.

I tell the guy to relax. This clinic is only for pregnant women and kids under five. The priority groups. Nobody else is getting anything. I've been holding this spot since four.

Tough, he says. Doesn't matter. Back of the line. No cutting.

I am too cold for this. Sick of him already.

You don't run this show, I say. This is our spot. I have been here since four and we're not going anywhere.

He steps in close to me. Tight. Smell the stale Tim Horton's on his breath. He whispers it in my ear.

Listen you little faggot, I got my own kid back there. She's freezing and now your guys are cutting in.

I know what it looks like, but it's not how it is.

It is how it is. No cutting.

The doors open and a nurse comes out, spots us instantly and understands. Must happen every morning. Ten times a day.

The guy tells her I'm trying to move my kids to the front.

I have been here since four.

She touches my arm and touches his arm at the same time. The voice is flat. No eye contact. Bureaucracy flows through her fluorescent bib. A performance of order no one can argue with.

There will be plenty for everyone, she says.

Lines that must come from a handbook.

Everyone will please return to their original spots. There will be plenty of vaccine. The staff of this clinic understand this is a stressful period for all families. We thank you in advance for your patience.

*

Henry IV's coronation in 1399. Most famous moment in the history of lice. The Archbishop, holding the crown in his hands, ready to set it on Henry's head. The granting of supreme power. Sees them, hundreds of lice, moving in the King's hair. Scared now to even touch him. Drops the crown and recoils. It nearly hits the floor. He backs away. Disgusted. Blessings extended from a distance. Lice in the palace, Henry spreads it through the entire court. Centuries of evasive tactics, but they cannot get away. Powdered wigs. Shaved heads underneath. Revolutions in hygiene. Zinsser tracks them all.

*

Dates and times printed out on small white cards. Where we need to be and when. Appointments and consultations. The doctors count our cells. Blood tests and urine tests. Semen samples. Vaginal discharge. What they tell us. There will never be kids. Impossible under these conditions. Levels bad on both sides. Figures that do not add up. Incompatible. A test we fail every month. Wait for it not to come, but the period arrives on time. Both know the expected day. She comes out of the bathroom. Closes the door. Shakes her head.

Twenty-six months of trying. More than two years. Like a wet fog, soaking through everything else. Folic acid supplements. Prenatal vitamins. No caffeine. The best odds diet. Cut down on the booze. Save yourself for when you are needed. A hidden calendar charts internal temperatures. Days with red X's and green X's. Ovulating. This is the window. Good cervical mucus is stretchy. Look at it, she says. A translucent elastic she pulls out of her body.

We go all the different ways. On the top and on the bottom. Pillow under the small of her back. Hands and knees. Standing up. Sitting down. Calculate angle and thrust. Deep and deep and deep. Hydraulics of life. Pressure and lubrication. Sweat dripping off the tip of my nose. Tears in her eyes. Salt water.

Desired outcomes. What we want is when we want it. No way to connect where we are and where we were. This is the opposite of everything we have ever done before. Sugar pills, place savers, in the circle dispenser. Click, click, click. Be sure to pull out. Blow your load. Days sprawling. Three years to finish the thesis. No rush. Smeared towels. Breakfast at three in the afternoon. Our first real bed, the mattress raised up off the ground. First place. Tall ceilings. Candles melting in the necks of wine bottles. Sticky cast off T-shirts. Summer humidity. Sun dresses and tank tops. Thin tan lines rolling over her shoulder. Freckles. Crusty Kleenex. A rubber swirling down the bowl. Ribbed for her pleasure. Random Wednesday afternoon. Lazy like you do not know.

How much do you think? she asks me once.

Blazing sunlight. Grey hand-job puddle in her palm. Devious, joking smile.

She holds it out. Slime on her fingers.

How much do you think? In one lifetime? How much can one guy produce? A pint of it? A gallon of splooge? No way. Think about that: a gallon, a milk jug in just one person? So, so, *so* gross.

What we will or will not do. She spits. It's like a spoonful of salty, spicy snot.

THEY PROVIDE US with choices. Second options. Back door solutions. Science and witch doctor stuff. In vitro. Voodoo remedies. Test tubes. Special teas. Surrogates. Yoga. Deep breathing. Are you too hot down there? Too tight? Forms to fill out for adoption. Somebody else's trip back from a Chinese orphanage. Maybe it will be just ourselves. And can you please tell me what would be so wrong with that? A clean house. Newspapers read cover to cover. Film festivals. Money. We might have money. Maybe just ourselves. Think about that for a second. Could we stay like this all the way through?

No, she says. No.

Twenty-six months of trying. But only twenty-six. Positive test result. Nobody can tell us why. Sometimes these things happen, they say. Sometimes. Zygote. Meiosis. Change. A series of diagrams I remember from a high-school Biology test. Still with me. Chromosomes pulling to the side, dividing on their own. Hold that stick directly in the stream of your urine. Wait for it. A mark emerging from the white background. Plus sign.

*

Zinsser. My crazed epidemiologist. How much I like him: "But the louse seems indefinitely committed to the materialistic existence, as long as lousy people exist. Each newborn child is a possible virgin continent, which will keep the louse a pioneer – ever deaf to the exhortations to better evaluate his values. If lice can dread, the nightmare of their lives is the fear of some day inhabiting an infected human being."

*

The night off. Home for Christmas and everybody else in bed. The baby goes down easy. Nervous energy from the road. Hit *The Bridge* with my brothers. Bring it on. Pitchers of draft and over-salted stale popcorn. There is never enough. Stay through to close. Rush to pay. This is on me. The next pitcher and a round of shots. Deep swallows and sour faces. Accept all obvious consequences for our actions. See the future. What is going to happen to us: Stagger back home, compete for couches. Sleep on the floor for two or three hours. Wake to the same hard morning. The world starting up again. My brain and your brain and your brain. Same hangover beating in every head. Know you will throw-up hours before you actually do.

Talk about nothing. Talk only for the voices, the sounds they make. The way they hold the table together. A good topic is all you need. Best nickname in the history of the Pistons.

Has to be The Worm.

Well, that sucks. He probably got it right there.

Might have to stop before we start.

You can't beat that. A professional athlete who called himself The Worm. We're talking the early Rodman here. Before the Bulls and the piercings and the multi-coloured hair. Before Madonna. Just a skinny freak of nature going up for the ball, boxing out guys six inches taller than he was. He gave up at least forty pounds every single night and still nobody could stop him. Defensive Player of the Year a million times. Crazy.

They had Spider Salley back there, too. All arms and legs. Coming off the bench. The front court was full of bug names.

James Buddha Edwards?

Nobody, nobody, worked the Fu Manchu better than that guy. It looked normal on him.

And you think Rodman was skinny, what about Tay Tay?

I like the way George Blaha says his name: "Tayshaun scoops it and he scores it."

Even Blaha kind of works when you think about it.

Yeah. Blaha is a possibility. You just leave it out there by itself: The Bla and then the Ha.

That's not a nickname, though, right? Blaha is his real name.

Fuck you.

Big Ben is too obvious. Swinging his sledgehammer with his homegame Afro teased all the way out.

'Let's go to work.' That was perfect.

Or Zeke. Remember when Isiah did those public service announcements for Detroit Edison. I guess they were trying cut down on accidental childhood electrocutions.

– Hey kids, look up.

– But, Isiah, I don't see anything.

– That's good, because there might have been power lines.

He was off the charts for the unintentionally hilarious.

Mahorn and Laimbeer. Evil sons of bitches. The real bad boys. Kept knocking Jordan on his ass for years and years before he got through.

And the new guys: Rip and Sheed and Chauncey.

Mr. Big Shot.

Rasheed bought an actual heavy-weight championship belt for every guy after they won. Said he'd take his five against any other five in the world.

He, Sheed, is the absolute greatest of all time. The G.O.A.T. Unstoppable whenever he felt like trying. Seven feet tall. Shooting the threes and taking the T's.

Best nickname in the history of the Pistons. Should have thought of it sooner: Vinnie Johnson.

A moment of silence. We nod our heads because this is true. There is no need to proceed.

Bigger than the Pistons, really, when you think about it.

Probably the best nickname in the history of sports.

Vinnie – *The Microwave* – Johnson.

Awesome.

It is *time* for the Microwave.

Remember that?

I most certainly do.

We need the Microwave right now.

His jump shot moved against the laws of physics.

How could that work? A line drive with no arc whatsoever.

I don't care how or why it worked. Just know it always went in.

Yep.

Put him in stone cold and he heats up to a scorching inferno in less than a second.

That's why they call him the Microwave.

Because he bringeth the heat.

Vinnie could sit on the bench for three and a half quarters doing nothing. He could be there in his street clothes and a pair of loafers, clapping his hands and telling jokes.

You put him in only when you need him.

Game on the line, down by four, three minutes left. Chuck makes the call.

Then, *Boom,* The Microwave goes off for 12 points down the stretch. He makes two threes and draws a charge on the other end. The starters sit to make room for him.

He's the guy who will walk to the line and sink both free throws to win it at the end, even when all the time has expired.

I want to propose a toast to the Microwave.

Yes. To Vinnie Johnson. For all he's given us.

To the Microwave for always delivering when it counted.

You can live a long, long time, but you will never see anything else like that.

*

Not the Romans or the Mongol hordes. Not Alexander, or the Crusaders, or the Spanish Armada, or Napoleon and the Nazis. No one was ever strong enough. All brought down in the end. This is Zinsser's true fascination. The history of the world indexed to the life of an insect: "this creature which has carried the pestilence that has devastated cities, driven populations into exile, turned conquering armies into panic-stricken rabbles." Lenin, during the revolution, millions dying around him. The outcome unsure. He doesn't know what is going to happen. It hangs in the balance. He says: Either socialism will defeat the louse or the louse will defeat socialism.

*

All the lights on in our house. Three in the morning. Something wrong. We come up the stairs and they are all waiting. She stands between my mother and father. The baby completely white now. Skin almost translucent. Purple eyelids. Lips dry and orange.

She threw up red, she says.

We have to go to the Hospital. You hold her and I'll drive.

Emergency room at Christmas time. Tree in the corner with a sign. *These gifts are empty boxes. Please refrain from opening.*

Rows of moulded seats with metal arm rails that make it impossible to lie down. A Saturday night crowd during the holidays. Woman with plastic bag socks. She has a shopping cart full of empty pop cans parked outside the sliding door. A guy sleeping across from us, legs splayed wide like an upside down "Y." Small separate bruises on the right side of his face. Ambulances rolling in and out. Stretchers. Overdoses. Bar fights. A man with a knife stuck right through his hand. Nurse tells him to leave it in and wait for further instructions. Triage.

We fill out our forms and huddle. Health Cards from a different province. Suspicion. You may have to pay for this up front and get reimbursed when you return home. Her temperature keeps rising. Wheezing when she breathes. Brown pus around her eyes. They take blood and urine samples right away. Then we wait.

Five hours. Six.

The light of the next day comes up. Regular staff arrive with coffee and their bagged lunches. Smile at each other. Talk about good two-for-one sales at the mall last night. The folding corrugated wall around the gift shop is opened up and the cash register blinks to life.

We take turns holding her. Passing the limp body back and forth. She hasn't opened her eyes all night. No sign of Vinnie Johnson.

Talk to them, she says. What is going on? They think they've called us. They think they've already called, but they haven't. They have our results by now. They have to have them. We've been here all night. Our file must be in the wrong place. Nobody would leave a baby out here, in this room, for an entire night at Christmas. Go talk to them.

At the desk, I say, do you think we can take our baby home, please, and maybe you can call us with the results? I don't think you fully understand the situation. We've been here for hours with a newborn and nothing is happening. Nobody has even checked on her.

At that moment, a doctor comes through the swinging doors and calls our name.

The nurse points at me.

Right there, she says. They want to know if they can go home.

He pulls the results out of a pile and looks me over. The same clothes for two days. The stink of the drive. No tooth-brush or razor. He can smell *The Bridge* all over me.

This child, he says, flipping the pages of the report, stretching it out. This child is not going anywhere.

He slams his clipboard down on the counter of the nurse's station. The swack brings the attention of the whole room onto my back. His eyes are furious. I am one of a hundred. There are a hundred every night. A thousand nights in a row.

This child, he says, and he points at her name, a purple impression on the top of a form, is very, very sick.

He waits. Breathes in and breathes out.

This child is seriously ill and she needs to be admitted to this hospital right away. She will be admitted into the paedi-atric intensive care unit. That is where she needs to be, sir. Not going home with you. We know what she needs. You, sir, you are the person who does not fully understand the situation.

We glare at each other. I sway in my own exhausted stench. Close my eyes for one second. I know what I look like.

Or I can call child services if you prefer, he says. We can start a file.

*

DDT was supposed to be the miracle cure. The end of Typhus and Malaria. Cheap and available everywhere. They sprayed it directly onto people's heads, into their armpits. Clothes fumigated. Whole houses. Beds, and pillows, and sheets. Utensils, cookware. Entire populations disinfected. They called it the pesticide that saved Europe. Guy got a Nobel Prize for inventing it. Total extermination. The side effects go unnoticed until it is too late. Already deep in the food chain. A half-life of 33 years in nature. Toxicity building up through each stage, passed from organism to organism. Ground water, rivers and lakes. Grains. Cash crops. Poultry and Fish and Reptiles. Endangered Species. Infected crocodiles and alligators, Bald Eagles and Peregrine Falcons. They lay eggs with thin, almost transparent shells. No protection. Causes infertility in humans. Breast cancer. Miscarriages. Low birth weight. Developmental delays. Numbers too high to count. But lice adapt. They go on. Become resistant. Completely unaffected by DDT now. Not like us. Trace amounts of it in every single person's blood.

*

Chronic kidney disease. Dangerously low filtration rate. Advanced infection. A congenital abnormality.

They strap the baby down. Immobilize her arm on a gauze-covered splint. A resident tries to find the vein for an infant IV. The nurse practitioner watches as the resident jabs and jabs again.

I can't find it, she says.

We are all watching.

It's always hard with small kids and babies. Just relax and try again. You'll get the hang of it eventually.

71

Two more misses. The resident bites the tip of her tongue. Another failed attempt.

We hold the baby's other hand. Pet her head. Everything will be okay. Her face contorts. She turns to look at us. Total confusion in her eyes. Betrayal. Why do you do this to me?

The nurse finally says, okay give it here. Then she misses three more times before something happens. She releases the tape and the medicine flows out of its plastic bag.

Make sure she doesn't pull that out.

She looks at me and I shake my head. They leave.

ULTRASOUNDS AND X-RAYS. Inject a dye into her bladder. Watch her pee on the monitor, the black colour running backwards, up through the malformed valve, snaking along the wrong path back to the shrunken kidney.

You see that? The technician says.

That is a high grade reflux with already extensive scarring. Lucky we caught it when we did. He pushes buttons. Screen captures for her file.

We try to take it all in. Get through to the essential information. Attempts at questions.

So what are we talking about here? I say. Is she going to be okay? How bad is it? We're not in transplant territory, are we?

She jumps in before he can say anything.

I could give her my kidney, right? One of us. We would have to be a good match. Then she could have a normal life. Be able to run around. I want her to be able to run around. Not sick all the time. We got it early enough, right? You can fix it. She's going to be fine.

I'm sorry, he says. I don't know anything. Just run the machine. The doctors interpret the results.

He checks his watch.

Have to wait and see. Could be severe complications or a simple procedure to fix the valve. Function might come right back to normal. You can't tell anything in the beginning. It doesn't look good now, but it all depends on how she responds. Could go any number of ways.

*

No sign of them for two weeks, but we can't be sure.

It's done, I say. They're gone. We made it.

Better be right this time, she says. Can't take much more.

My brain still teeming. The itch. It doesn't require proof or evidence. Thought is enough. You do it to yourself. Lice. Imagine them crawling on your head. Claws touching skin. They pass over us, across this family.

I wander the quiet house at night. Think I sense them everywhere, penetrating cushions and clothes and blankets. No place too intimate. Asleep in our bed. Her head against the pillowcase, hair fanned out. The girl with the Clash T-shirt. We get to choose each other, but kids have no say about the nature of their own lives. Two girls and a boy. Dead to the world. Separate beds. Each clutching a stuffed animal. What are we to these people? Genetics. A story they make up about themselves.

Can't sleep without the stuffies. Essential part of the night time ritual. Sacred objects made in a Bangladesh factory. The soft places where children dump their love for the first few years. Think of the crying and the frantic searches. What happens to us if one of these toys gets lost or left behind at the grocery store.

But the lice creep in. Even here. Wait it out for a chance to come back. I take the battered elephant and the patched monkey and the frayed horse. Pry them out of the kids' arms without waking anybody up. Bring them downstairs to the basement. Toss everybody into the deep freezer for the night. They sleep on a value pack slab of frozen pork chops. The only treatment guaranteed to kill.

This is what I have learned from Hans Zinsser. Lice need a regular temperature. Can't survive extreme shifts. Sensitive to the smallest change in the host. They can tell when it is time to move on. The writing on the wall. A bad fever sometimes enough. Lice know what you don't. Leave a body voluntarily the second it starts to cool. People who have lived through cataclysms – veterans from the war, victims of earthquakes, those who escaped the camps – they will tell you. Lice, like a cloud, like ink, seeping from the head and the groin of a corpse. Confirmation. They register it first, the cold taste, the stillness. Bodies on the ground, dropped in the exercise yard, leaking their insects.

*

We take it in shifts. Not smart to burn out two people at the same time. The room has one chair that can fold out into a very narrow single bed. One sits up with the baby, while the other goes home and tries to sleep. My turn, then your turn. Rotation. We pass in the hall sometimes. Exchange Tupperware meals. Concerned families waiting in different houses. The news. What the doctor said this time. Nothing happened today. She had a good night.

Medication. The baby wakes up, starts to come back to herself. Little by little. Gurgling and happy sometimes, but not out of the woods. She reaches out through the metal bars of the hospital crib. Holds my finger.

They have her hooked up to a machine. Tubes and wires. A long strip of paper, like a sales slip, scrolling out. Something inside draws a continuous erratic line over the narrow graph paper. It goes up and down. Sometimes rests for a long plateau. The nurses consult it every time they come in the room. We have no idea what it means. When we ask, they say: more data for the chart. There are numbers, too. Three of them. Two for blood pressure, we think, and then something else. A single flashing light, but no sound. The bulb is purple. Blinks on and off. Fluctuates. A silent rhythm, picking up and coming back down. Her heart, most likely, but it seems too slow sometimes.

I come to relieve her. 10:30 at night. Freezing outside. Other things will happen, but we will never live clearer than this. I take off my boots. She puts hers on. Car outside waiting in temporary parking. Meter running. The heater will stay warm if we switch fast enough.

She just went down, she says. Probably be up for something to eat in two or three hours. New bottle of formula in the fridge at the nurse's station.

Okay, good. There's spaghetti waiting for you.

I hold her. All her weight collapses into me and we both cry. Quiet empty corridors in the hospital. Nothing happening. All the overhead lights turned down.

When are they going to let us go?

I don't know. Have to wait till they say something.

She puts on her winter coat. Turns to leave.

I move to the chair. The upholstery is hard blue vinyl. Cleaning staff wipe it down every morning with a spray bottle of disinfectant. I push it back so the recliner part kicks up. It is about two-feet wide, hard metal support bars running below the surface. You can go down, maybe, but you cannot sleep here. The place where you wait for the next day to come.

I get one of the thin pillows from the shelf in the bathroom. Look up and see her at the end of the hall. Waiting by the elevator. Her head shaking. The numbers descending. I call her name as I move, almost run, down the corridor in my sock feet. Meet her on the way. Kiss.

Stay, I say.

Please stay.

She smiles.

We go back. Squeeze onto the vinyl chair. Her legs between my legs. Arms hanging over the side. Heads touching. Everything forced together. Darkness in the room. Our baby makes no sound. Only the bulb from the machine now. Inscrutable purple light flashing on the ceiling. Like a discotheque, maybe, or the reflection of ancient fire in a cave.

Light Lifting

Nobody deserved a sunburn like that. Especially not a kid. You could see it right through his shirt. Like grease coming through waxed paper. Wet and thick like that, sticking to him. Purple. It was a worn out, see-through shirt and the blisters he had from the day before had opened up again. Now they were hardening over for the second time, sucking the fabric into his back. I tried not to think about him taking that shirt off. He'd have to rip at it quickly – like a bandage – and that would tear away any of the healing that had already happened. Half his back would go. He had a sunburn bad enough to bleed.

I saw it coming the day before and I probably should have said something and stopped it. It was bright. One of those clear afternoons where there's just enough of a breeze to trick you into thinking it's nice and cool. On a day like that you can forget that the sun is still up there, on top of the breeze, still coming straight down. Most people have been caught at least once by a trick day like that and it's worse now. Now it's over before you feel anything. You can get permanently hurt if you don't pay attention.

I watched it happen. I watched that burn going into him – the pink blotches moving across his shoulders and down the backs of his arms. He was turning colours right in front of me and I didn't say a word. Instead, I thought about how it's strange that you really can't feel a burn like that when it's going in. Or you feel it only like a nice comfortable kind of all-over warm. Everything seems fine when you're out there in the daytime, but at night – when a bad burn starts to come out – that's a totally different thing. That's a special kind of trouble. I've been there. Probably everyone's been there.

First it's nothing. You flip over on your stomach and just try to stay still. You pick that one steady position and try to hold it. But it gets worse, and even though you take the cold bath and pile on the noxema, you still think you're going to come bursting right out of your own body. Your skin feels too tight. In the end you have to give up on sleeping because now it's four in the morning and you can see the sun coming up for another round. Every time you breathe there's a separate stretching pain.

I let him burn because I thought I'd never see him again. But when he came back the next morning – when he came back again, all scorched like that but still ready to go – that turned me around on him for good. I felt sorry for him now and I kept thinking that some of this was my fault. I felt like I did it to him myself – held him down and poured boiling water all over his back or pushed a plugged-in iron onto his skin. He had no way of knowing what he was getting into. His name was Robbie.

When Robbie came back on that second morning he didn't talk to anyone. He just did what he was told and kept nodding his head all the time. But at about eleven, when the real heat started up and the other guys had their shirts off, it looked to me like he was going to try again. I saw him tugging at the neck of his T-shirt, thinking about it.

"For fuck's sake," I said. "Just sweat it out for a couple days. You take that shirt off today, you'll be in the hospital by tomorrow night. I guarantee you'll be in the hospital."

That was the first thing I ever said to him.

"It's okay," he said. His voice was flat and calm, like he already had this all figured out.

"I'm prepared for it today," he said. "I bought sunscreen last night. A sixty-five. Nothing can get through that. I'm ready for it today."

"Sixty-five." He said that again, slowly, stretching it out. Like he was amazed. Like sixty-fucking-five was the biggest number in the history of the world.

"Never knew they went that high," he said.

He had the lotion in his backpack and he took it out and showed it to me. There were two palm trees growing out of a little yellow island on the bottle. He wanted to do it right there. Take off his shirt and reach around and slather himself up. He took off his gloves, wiped the dust off his hands.

"Wouldn't go like that if I were you," I said. "That shit will be worse than anything the burn can do. Oil in your hands doesn't go with bricks."

He looked at me like I was joking with him.

"Do what you want," I said. And I held up my hands like I surrendered.

"I'm only telling you the two things don't go together. When that grease sinks in, you can't get it out. Not like it's sticky, but it gets right in there and messes up your hands. Softens them. Makes the skin split. Doesn't even hurt at first when your fingers start bleeding, just feels wet. But by the end, your palms are all shredded up and the tips are worn right off your fingers. Goes right through your gloves."

Everything I told him was true. When you wreck your hands they never come back the same way. I got my fingers so bloody and infected once that when they finally healed over again I could still see little chunks of stone trapped under my skin.

Robbie kind of smiled and he shook his head back and forth. He put the cream back in his bag.

"No lotion," he said. Then he looked straight at me and for a second I thought he was going to quit right there. I could see two little veins pulsing in the middle of his forehead. But he didn't go for it. He looked up at the sky like he was trying to figure out if there was a better place to stand – a place with some shade.

"They say it's supposed to be very hot today," he said.

"Yes," I told him. "That's what I heard."

WE HAD A STRANGE MIX of guys on our crew that year. There were just three regulars – me, JC and Tom – and then we had summer kids who rotated in and out, a different one almost every day. Tom was our foreman. He did the estimates, set up the jobs and made sure that everything kept moving. JC and I laid in most of the stone.

The letters JC stood for Jesus Christ. His real name was Allan but we called him JC because he was born again. Before he came back to real life JC was a paratrooper in the military. He used to jump out of planes. His skin was covered with the kind of tattoos you can only get in the army or in jail. He had the regular naked-woman kind and a couple skulls and some crucifixes with snakes slithering around them. But he had the harder stuff too. Amateur tattoos that looked like a kid had drawn them in. There were a lot of shaky words written out on JC's body. Some of them were spelled wrong and sometimes the spacing was too tight and you could tell that they had to squish to get all those little sayings to fit inside their separate curling flags. On his back he had a picture of a bomb that was tied up to its own little parachute. It said "Death Comes From Above." And there was another one that stretched right across the back of his neck, right over the bone of his spine. He had his old unit number there and the little flag said "Pain Is Unavoidable." But somebody mixed up the O and the I, so it really said "Pain Is *Unaviodable.*"

JC was a little bit off. Something bad happened to him, I think. Maybe it was in those war simulations or something in the training that's supposed to break a guy down into just his basic parts. Once, Tom asked JC if he was sure that his parachute opened every time he jumped out of the plane. Tom acted it out for JC. He whistled a windy high note when he thought about JC falling through the air and then he slapped his hands together hard when he thought about him hitting the ground.

"Come on," Tom said. "Think back. That happened to you at least one time. Whatever it was, you had to get whacked pretty hard to turn out like this."

JC squinted a lot, like he was always staring into a lamp that was too bright. But I don't have a bad word to say about him. The guy was completely sound around me except for all his talking about God and the holy scriptures and the coming of the Rapture or whatever. He could really work too, almost like he was powered by the Almighty Lord or some other crazy magic. He could just go and go and go, no matter what time it was, or how hot it was, or if it was raining, or if it was snowing. During his lunch hour he prayed and he read the Bible to us out loud.

The guy was carved up so tight it was like the muscles in his back and his stomach were drawn in with the tattoos. When he took off his shirt, he looked like the worst sort of criminal: the kind in the prison movies who do hundreds of push-ups and sit-ups in their cells. It bothered some of our customers to have him around. The young married couples with kids and minivans didn't want a guy like that working in front of their new houses. JC had a special feel for those kind of people. He could sense them. When somebody looked at him like that, he never let it pass. He always wanted to talk to them, explain his whole life story. Tell them how he'd been transformed.

"You do not need to be afraid of me," he'd say.

One time he started talking like that to a guy who was watering his lawn while we put in his driveway. The man had been staring at us for a couple of minutes and I remember that he was wearing a green golf shirt and he didn't have any shoes on.

Right out of the blue JC said to him, "You can change yourself, you know. It doesn't have to be this way."

He talked with that funny up and down rhythm that the black preachers have.

"We can change ourselves," he said. "Just look at me. You have to look if you want to see."

And then he turned around so the man could read the words and see the pictures on his back.

"I am the proof," JC said. "I am the proof that you can change. This is the skin of a different man. This is just a shell to remind me of how it used to be. But I am saved now. And you. You can be saved too."

The guy with the golf shirt just stood there and nodded his head. I don't think there was anything else for him to do. The hose kept dripping water on the grass and JC kept turning himself around. From where I was standing, I couldn't tell if the barefoot guy was having a religious experience or not.

Tom tried to smooth things out after that. Whenever he talked to customers Tom was always professional. He told the barefoot guy that we apologized for the inconvenience and that it would never happen again and that we could discuss a discount or something. But later, when I saw him whispering with JC, Tom was back to himself. There was spit foaming at the corners of his mouth.

"You ever do that again," he said to JC, "and you're gone."

Tom was trying to keep himself together, trying to keep it low, but I could hear him breathing hard out of his nose and I could see the way he was trembling all over when he talked. For a second, I thought he might actually haul off and punch JC right there in this guy's backyard. I was thinking that that would have been good for our reputation.

"We'll dump you so fast it'll make your head spin," Tom told JC. "And then what'll you do? Where would you go then? Nobody else would take you."

Our company worked guys who couldn't get any other kind of work. Garlatti, our boss, he looked for people like JC and like Tom. Guys who were desperate for a job or stuck because of something they did a long time ago. I worked with Tom for years but I never found out what happened with him. I heard he beat somebody up. Somebody close to him. His wife or his girlfriend or one of his kids, I think, from before. He lived by himself now but I think he still had to pay out almost all the money he made. Tom had to take lots of days off because he was always going to court or to these meetings with some officer who was supposed to keep track of him.

I ate my lunch with Tom every day and every day it was the same thing. At exactly 11:30 he'd go to the back of the truck and haul out his little red cooler. He'd open it up, bring out the cold six-pack, and then he'd drink every one of them in less than half an hour. In all that time, I never saw the guy eat food during lunch. And every day – every single day that we worked together – he made a point of offering that last beer to me, just because he knew I had to stay away from that stuff.

"Come on, Jimmy," he'd say and he'd wave the last can in front of me. Back and forth and then back and forth another time. "What the hell difference does it make now. You're past all that."

In the beginning Garlatti paid us absolutely nothing. But every once in a while he softened up a bit. He used to give us these secret raises that we weren't supposed to tell anybody about. One week your check would be fifty or seventy-five dollars bigger and when he handed it to you he'd give the paper a little extra push into your hand so that you'd know not to open it in front of everybody else. That's how he kept his regulars for so long. We kept coming back every week, waiting for that extra fifty bucks to show up.

IT WAS DIFFERENT for the kids though. Garlatti paid them the straight minimum wage and he never budged on that. The man never paid out one cent more than he had to. In the beginning, some of the students tried to pretend that hauling bricks was simply good exercise. Like they figured that if they had to work a bad summer job then they might as well get a tan or get in shape when they were doing it. Guys like that never lasted. Before we got Robbie, Tom must have hired and fired 50 kids, almost one a day since the beginning of the summer.

The job was simple. Carrying bricks, that was it. Carrying bricks all day long and shovelling a little gravel here and there. The kids had to run new brick off the pallets and wheelbarrow away the scraps and the cut pieces. It was their job to keep us stocked up all the time so that me and JC could lay it in nonstop. At first, most of them thought the job couldn't be that hard. But when we needed to, me and JC could lay it down pretty quick. Back and forth, as fast as fast. Somedays, if we got a feeling for it, we could knock off three driveways or maybe five backyard patios.

The kids usually came out in the morning, worked with us for a day, and then quit when we brought them back in the afternoon. It was the best thing for all of us. They didn't even come back at the end of the week to pick up their money. Garlatti was smart. He probably pulled a couple hundred hours of free work from that one little piece of paper he had stuck to a bulletin board down at the employment centre. It was like we had a never ending supply of kids to break down.

But Robbie was the last one we hired that summer. He started on the fifteenth of June and he worked right through to the beginning of September. His sunburn cleared up after a while. For the first couple weeks, when his skin was peeling off, he looked kind of scaly, like he was changing into some sort of lizard guy from a screwed-up experiment, but by the end of the summer he was back to normal. He never took off his shirt again though, so I don't know what kind of scars he got left with.

"Look at him," Tom said to me once.

It was on that second day, in the afternoon, and Robbie was running, I mean really running, with these bricks. He piled them up between his arms and carried them in stacks of seven or eight. He held the bottom one with his fingers and the top one tucked in just under his chin. Robbie moved with these quick jerky steps. There was nothing smooth about him. He was always halfway between standing up and crouching down.

Anyone who's ever done this kind of work can tell you that the bending over is the worst part of it. Bending over and getting up, and then bending over and getting up again – it's like you're folding and unfolding your body all day. You get creaky. And just that little bit of weight – just the weight that's in a couple bricks – that's enough to grind you down. Any kid can pick up a hundred pounds if they only have to do it one or two times. But it's the light lifting that does the real damage. Maybe it's just thirty pounds and it starts off slow, but it stays with you all day and then it hangs around in your arms and your legs even after you leave. That kind of lifting hits you in the knees first and then in your shoulders and your neck. It used to surprise our summer student kids. It would catch them off-guard, usually in the early afternoon, just after lunch. One minute they'd be loud and laughing and tossing the brick around like it was nothing and then, all of a sudden, that little grinding pain would wind up and get a hold of them. You could almost see it tightening around them. It was like they got old all at once. They'd hunch over and get really quiet and start concentrating on the smallest things, trying to figure out what went wrong.

But Robbie ran the brick faster than we could lay it down. Sometimes he'd have to wait for us to catch up and he'd stand there watching everything we did. For him, it was like putting in a driveway was important work. After a month I think we forgot that this wasn't his real life and that he was just passing through.

"He's the best guy we ever had for that job," JC told me. "It's like he has a gift. He loves it."

Robbie worked with us during the crazy time when the city was growing all day and all night and there was more work than anyone could do. I'm glad I don't live in a house that went up at that time because it was all speed more than it was doing it right. If you could swing a hammer and carry a two-by-four, you were framing houses.

Garlatti overbooked us a lot. When we had too many jobs, the work we did was never very good. We were always rushing to get to the next place and we cut a lot of corners. When it slowed down and there was nothing coming up, then we took our time. We stretched everything as far as it would go.

I liked to get it right. Make it perfect. I liked the one-of-a-kinder jobs. Like when some lady wanted us to put a connecting circle pattern in her back patio. We could do that. Or when a guy wanted to write out his initials in the stone of his driveway. People asked us to do that kind of stuff for them. They wanted a big capital M in there with a different colour brick.

I know that most people don't pay attention to paving stone when they're walking on it, but they don't know how hard it is to do something like that. When you're laying down a special job, you gotta be able to see the end before you can start. I stayed up all night sometimes with a piece of graph paper, trying to figure out how to put some stupid "Q" in there and still make everything else fit.

Once when we were doing a job like that – putting in the connecting circles – Robbie asked me to show him how to do it. He wanted to know how I made the whole thing come together.

I took out my paper from the night before and I showed him how to draw out the circles with a compass and how to colour in the squares where they overlapped. I told him about how you always had to keep it balanced when you were laying it in.

"When you do something on one side, then you got to do it on the other side too," I said. "You gotta make two circles at the same time."

I showed him how to cut the small pieces so you didn't waste any brick and how to bring the curve around slowly so it looked natural.

Robbie's eyes flicked between the paper and the patio we were building. I could see that he was really studying this stuff. Figuring it out. He'd ask me a question and I'd answer and we went back and forth like that. It was great. Before that, I never taught anybody anything.

WE HARDLY EVER GOT TO DO that kind of speciality work though. It was too expensive and it took too long to set up. When we were busy, it was pure assembly line. Churning through it. Never much of anything unique. If I wanted to slow down because something was a bit off, or I wanted to show Robbie how to get around a tricky corner, Tom would start yelling at us and say, "For Chrissake, just give it a whack and make it fit. It's construction here, you're not building no watch."

We spent most of our time in the new subdivisions. Southwood Lakes, Castlepoint, Elmwood. They all had names like that. It was a goldmine for Garlatti. The houses were all the same and every one of them needed a big two-car driveway in the front and a little circle patio for the barbecue in the back. We stormed from one lot to the next, building all these driveways onto the empty street.

There were other companies in there too. With their own trucks and their own names painted on the side. Roofers and electricians and plumbers. Everybody was making money then. They were building the big wooden decks, or putting in the Jacuzzi bathtubs and the automatic garage door openers. The other kind of summer kids were there too. The ones who started their own landscaping companies. They were always under our feet, trying to carry around their rolls of sod and those big bags of wood chips. Southwood Lakes was the fanciest of all those places. There was a big brown wall that went all the way around it and was supposed to keep out the noise from the highway. Every one of those houses had a view of the lakes.

We were working out there when they actually dug those lakes and it was like nothing I ever saw. A surveyor went around with a can of special spray paint and he took some readings and then drew these gigantic weird bendy shapes on the ground. Took him about a week to get it done. One time, I met him at the canteen truck and asked him how it was going and he said that they'd start digging tomorrow. The next day they came in with the heavy machinery and just followed the lines, like a cut-out in a colouring book, five feet deep all the way across.

"See that," I said to Robbie, "I guess that's how you make a lake."

But that was it. One week it was grass, the next week it was water. And everybody had a view. They put a filter system in there, like a swimming pool, so that the lake didn't get all swampy. Southwood was supposed to be a nice place to live. Nice if you had kids.

When they first filled those Southwood Lakes with water, JC took off all his clothes and swam around in there naked. He dove down and showed us his completely unmarked ass. And he kept calling to us to come out there and join him. He would baptize us again, he said, in the name of the Father, and the Son, and the Holy Spirit, Amen. Robbie and I just laughed at him. We were sitting in the shade of a big tree that hadn't even been there two days before. But Tom didn't think it was so funny. He grabbed himself through his jeans and yelled out that if JC wanted to see him naked he could walk right up here and suck his dick.

WE NEVER REALLY KNEW OUR CUSTOMERS. Sometimes the driveways we were building were going onto houses that hadn't even been sold yet. Everything was empty out there. Like a ghost town in the middle of a field, but full of mansions.

Once in a while we'd get a renovation job back in the old part of the city and when we came back to the normal streets we could see all the differences. There was traffic and all the houses were different shapes and there were kids and dogs everywhere.

We were doing a job like that when the old lady who hired us recognized Robbie.

"Is that you Robert," she said. You could tell she was uncertain, kind of like she couldn't believe it.

All of us looked up at the same time because it was strange to have a customer talking right to us. But here was this lady and she was calling him Robert. He smiled at her.

"Yes, it's me," he said. "How are you?"

"Oh, I'm good, I'm good," she said. "Just coming back from the school. Getting ready for the new year. Lots of preparation to do, you know." She had a bag full of papers.

"This is it for you, right?" she said. "You'll be graduating this year."

"Yes," Robbie said. "This is it. One year left."

In the back of my head I always knew that Robbie and most of the other kids who worked with us were still only in high school, but I never really thought about it before. It threw me a bit, seeing him talk to that lady about graduating and school sports teams and calculus classes. I looked over at JC and then at Tom. I thought about JC saying his prayers at night and how Tom and I would go home and cook ourselves a dinner and then sit there in front of the TV and watch a ball game. For me, it'd been like that for so long, I think I stopped wondering about how it could be different for anybody else. Robbie was probably seventeen years old. What did a kid like that do when he went home? You could spend all this time working with a guy and still be totally different inside. I thought about how we were all stuck, all of us put in our places. I thought about how your life could be like a brick and how it was hard to move it once you got settled into the same place for a couple years.

"So this is your summer job, then," the lady said.

She looked at us and smiled and then she said to JC – like she was joking with him – "I hope you fellas aren't working him too hard. Robert is one of the best. You take care of him, okay?"

"We will," JC said quickly. He talked in that same over-keen way that people use when they're trying to impress their teachers. "We'll take care of him."

She went into her house and then five minutes later she came out with a big pitcher of lemonade for all of us.

"Robert," she said. "When you have your break, why don't you come inside for a bite of lunch?"

He stopped for a second, but it wasn't like he needed to think about it. Everything that came out of that boy's mouth came out natural.

"Thanks," he said. "But I can only come if we all go."

She was a little surprised, but she was quick on her feet and she rolled right along with it.

"Oh of course, of course," she said. "That's what I meant. There's room for all of you."

And that's how it happened. Robbie and me and JC and Tom ended up sitting around the kitchen table with this old lady. Eating her tuna fish sandwiches with the crusts cut off and the Oreo cookies and the big glasses of milk. JC got down on his knees and said grace beside the table. He thanked God for the food and for bringing us all together and for keeping us healthy. And the lady kept filling up our glasses and bringing more cookies. Every once in a while, Robbie and I would glance back at each other smiling our heads off. Tom just sat there, completely quiet. I think he was wishing for his little red cooler. It was all I could do not to burst out laughing. Quite the scene. We were like the opposite of one big happy family.

ON THE LAST FRIDAY that Robbie worked with us, we all decided to quit early. We'd been going like mad for nearly three months, six or seven days a week, and Garlatti decided that we could take the half-day. So we knocked off right at twelve noon and we decided that we'd take Robbie out for lunch because we didn't know when we were going to see him again. He was starting school again the next week.

"If you ever need a job, we got one for you," Tom said. It was probably the only nice thing I ever heard him say.

"You can make good money in this business," he said. It was like he was trying to convince himself.

"There's lots of side jobs, lots of under-the-table stuff. Opportunities all around. You should think about it."

Robbie said that he would.

We took him to this bar called the Silver Bullet. Tom picked the place. He said they had good lunch specials. The sign for the Silver Bullet had a cartoon girl wearing a little skimpy bikini top and she was riding on a big silver bullet. She had a cowboy hat that she waved in the air while she smiled her big smile. They didn't charge us anything, or even check Robbie for ID, because it was still so early and that kind of business didn't get going until much later on. It took a while for my eyes to adjust to the mirrors and the strobe lighting and the rest of it. It took a while before I could see.

The only other people in there were the staff and then this other big group of guys wearing matching blue coveralls. I think they were a road crew because their clothes were all covered in black tar and they smelled like asphalt. There were probably ten of them.

"City workers," Tom said and he snorted. "They need twenty guys to fill in a pot hole."

We ordered some food and JC bought everybody a round of beer and a ginger ale for me. We sat there all quiet. It was like none of us even knew how to talk. There was an afternoon ball game on so we watched that and once in a while somebody would say something after a nice catch or a double play. We ate the burgers, and they drank their beers. And then Tom bought a round, and I bought a round, and even Robbie bought a round. Then it started again. The waitress kept bringing the bottles and taking them away. After a while I started to feel a little rough because I can't sit in a bar for too long. They had all the hard stuff right out in the open. The bottles were lined up behind the counter. I watched Robbie drinking his beers and laughing with those guys and it made me feel kind of sick, like I was doing something wrong. I was just jumpy, I suppose, but I could tell it wasn't good.

Then Tom got up to go to the john. When he walked past the guys from the road crew, I saw him lean over their table and say something to them. I knew right then that there was going to be trouble. There were more of them than us, they'd been here longer than us, and they'd gone through more rounds.

One of the guys on the other side of the table got up and he started waving and shouting at Tom, telling him to fuck off and just move along. I prayed that Tom would just shut up but I knew he couldn't. With Tom, it was instinct. He was like a Pitbull. It didn't matter how long he'd been nice because one day he'd just have turn on you. There was a pure meanness inside of him that he couldn't do anything about.

I heard Tom say something about the union and about how these guys had never done a day of real work in their lives. He spit on the floor. Then two more of the men were standing up and they were trying to separate Tom from the guy who was yelling at him. They each tried to take hold of one of his arms and lead him away. Another guy looked over at us and kind of waved so that we'd come and get him. But it was too late. Tom pushed one of those guys off him and he tripped and fell into the table and the glasses spilled and bottles were breaking.

"Fucking pussies," Tom shouted. "You're all a bunch of pussies."

Then the guy behind Tom hit him over the head with a full bottle of beer and he went down.

JC was across the room so fast, I didn't even see him move. He was over there in one second. And there were two more blue overall guys there to meet him but they couldn't stop it. It was like JC just flicked a switch in his head and he was back to being the kind of guy he looked like. He went right for the one who hit Tom with the beer bottle. In one swoop JC was over the table and he swung at the guy so hard that when his hand came into the other guy's face the guy's nose just exploded. JC had his whole body behind that punch. When he came up on the other side, JC had blood on his face but I knew it wasn't his.

Robbie and I started to go over and some of them came to get us. It was like we were all in this game and everybody knew the rules and everybody needed to be partnered up. The staff were screaming at us, calling us all drunk pieces of shit and trying to push the whole thing outside into the parking lot. During all of this – even when one of the coverall guys with a big ring on his finger smashed his hand into the space right between my nose and my eye – I kept wondering how we could have made this not happen on Robbie's last day. At the same time, I was thinking that it couldn't be avoided.

When we came out into the back parking lot I saw Tom lying balled up on the ground. There was blood coming out of one of his ears. Two of the blue overall guys were taking turns kicking him in the head and in the ribs with their big boots.

Another guy ran up to me and put his two hands on my shoulders. Then he pulled me forward and jammed his knee up as hard as he could right square between my legs. I felt something tearing and I went down. The two guys left Tom to go for somebody else behind me, but I couldn't get up and I couldn't breathe right and I couldn't turn around.

Tom wasn't moving anymore. He just lay there, face up, on the hot asphalt, between the yellow lines of a parking spot. It was so warm. We'd only been in there for a couple hours and it was still very early in the day, probably not even three o'clock yet. The sun just kept streaming down on us, all bright and summery. It wasn't right and I kept wishing for it to be darker so I didn't have to see it all so clearly.

Adult Beginner I

There is a sequence to follow. Two steps.

Mel explains it again.

"You go all the way out," she says. "Then all the way down."

She points over the edge and into the dark. Very specific. As if there is only one spot, a particular place in the sky, you have to reach before you can turn and head for the water. Her arm sways through an up-and-down roller coaster motion. "You swan dive it, right? Out first, then down. Know what I mean?"

The wind picks up and pushes them both forward. Up here, the air feels colder than it did before and the bugs are bad. Stacc waves a swarm away from her nose. Down below, a thin layer of mist smokes above the water.

Mel pulls back another swallow from her Wildberry wine cooler and circles her thumb and finger around the clear neck of the bottle. She is still wet from the last time and uses her foot to re-smear the line on the roofing tar. It is two-thirty in the morning, but the tar or the melted tires or whatever toxic black substance they use to coat the roof is warm and spongy, holding on to the heat from the day.

"Right from here," she says. "Then fast as you can until, bang, you hit the side and you're gone." There's a hard stomp in the middle of her instructions.

"And when you're out there, you put your hands wide like this, like you're flying. Like one of those cliff divers in

Mexico. And you keep your chin way, way up and you keep moving out, out, out as far as you can. Then when you feel the out giving up, you pull a quick tuck and go for the water."

Mel moves her whole body as she acts it out. Her chin strains upward, arms stretched to a capital T. Then a complete creasing fold at the waist, palms flattening on the roof. Fluorescent pink wine cooler foams in her bottle like radioactive potion. Her hips and shoulders, all her limbs and joints, move loose and graceful and drunk. She is unstoppable.

"If you get mixed up," she says, trying to steady her stare into Stace's eyes, trying to make the words come out separately, one-by-one, and clear.

"If you get mixed up, remember the lights are blinking inside the river. That's the water, right? Not the sky. The lights are reflecting inside the river and you reach down into the lights. Don't get lost and get yourself all turned around or you end up belly-flopping or just falling straight off the side."

"Down to the light," Stace nods. "Right."

"Some people use the buildings on the other side. They look at the Renaissance Center and keep themselves in line with that. I think you're supposed to dive down like you're following the elevators. Doesn't matter really. Just keep track of where you are and make sure you go in smooth."

There are seven of them up here on the roof of the hotel – four guys and three girls – and everyone else has already done it two or three times. It is nothing new. Kids have been jumping from this spot, the top of the Waterfront Holiday Inn, for years. The Odeon movie theatre is connected, built right into the hotel, and not long ago the two sets of owners were supposed to hook up and hire some extra security to finally put a stop to this kind of stuff, but nothing really changed. They only had enough money for a weekend guy and this is a

Tuesday. Stace knows they will not be caught. Nobody is going to climb up that ladder and stop this from happening.

The routine is simple. They start behind the line and sprint to the edge and scream as they take the last step and disappear headfirst into the dark. Then there's a long, long moment of quiet and then the splash. After that, more waiting, a second long second of quiet, and then the surfacing, followed by screaming and clapping and shouting. Somebody always says *Hoe-lee Fuck* and somebody else always says *Unfuckingbelievable*.

Stace is going to do it, too. Doing is the only thing left. But it will have to happen soon. There are reasons not to, of course, obvious ones, but they seem flimsy and unconvincing right now and in the end every risk has to be measured relative to doing nothing at all. She feels it coming, though. The advance presence of a killer threat. Real danger waiting off to the side. It swirls around them like faint smoke drifting in from an approaching forest fire, but nobody else cares. What are the chances? It is the middle of summer, the night after a sunny day, and the wind is the only thing that demands real attention. A bad gust at the wrong time could mess with your trajectory during the sixty-foot drop. One of the guys sucks back a wad of phlegm and gobs over the side to test what happens to his spit on the way down.

"WHAT DOES IT TASTE LIKE?"

"What do you mean, *taste?*"

"The water. What does it taste like? I always thought the river would taste like chemicals or like gasoline. Stingy and hot, like Javex or something you can light on fire. Know what I mean? From all the pollution and the pesticides and the factories? Does it taste like that? Does the water taste like oil?"

"No," Mel says. "What are you talking about?" She shakes her head, tired of the stalling.

"It tastes like nothing, like water. I wouldn't drink a gallon of it, but come on. Compared to the pool, compared to what we work in everyday, it seems pretty clean and natural to me. Totally fine. And it's a river, not a lake. It's just passing through, not sitting around waiting and collecting all that crap. I like the way it moves you and moves around you. You can feel the current pushing when you're in there and you have to swim hard to get back to the side or it'll just drag you away. You'll see. When you do it, when you're in there, it's no big deal."

Going over the side is not the hardest part and every-body knows there are other problems. Like they say there's supposed to be a homeless guy, some paranoid schizo-phrenic, who has made it his life's work to toss a bunch of old shopping carts down here, right into the middle of the diving spot. He's been doing this for years and they say there are probably fifty or a hundred-and-fifty of them down there by now, a tangled pile of steel rods and rusting wheels, waiting in the water for some kid to come slicing down head-first.

Stace thinks about fold-down shopping cart seats, the places where babies ride as they go up and down the aisles. There's a thick handle, a basic hinge, the plastic flap and two square holes where the legs stick out. The carts are designed to be shoved into each other. Their back panels detach and flip up when they link. She spins one of them in her mind, repositions it tilted forward, standing vertical in the water, a couple of inches below the surface. The panel yawns open like a metal mouth. This is why you have to go out before you go down. To get beyond the range of even the most revved-up psycho's cart-slinging ability.

"It's fucking freezing," Mel says. "One more and I'm done. I have to teach my Aquakids at nine in the morning."

She hugs herself, arms X'd across her chest, an open palm rubbing the opposite shoulder. When she stops to bring the bottle back to her mouth, Stace can see Mel's hand shaking and hear the bones of her teeth banging against the glass before she gets her lips around the circle and swallows again.

Mel pulls a thin towel over her shoulders and tries to wrap it around her blue, city-issued Lifeguard bathing suit with the Parks and Rec logo stencilled just above her hip bone. Eight hours ago, she was singing *If you're happy and you know it, splash your hands* and blowing motorboat bubbles and splaying her arms and legs out as far as they could go to make a good starfish float. But then the evening teaching lines ended and all the kids went home and the Tuesday crew geared up for its regular run.

That's what they call themselves. The Tuesday crew. After the kid's lessons from six to seven-thirty and the grown-up classes from seven-thirty to eight-fifteen and the lengths swim from eight-fifteen to nine-thirty, the pool empties out and the Lifeguards have the place to themselves. When the last customers clear the changing rooms, they lock the front doors and make sure they're alone. Then they reach into the zippered side pockets of their gym bags, unfold their protective, cushioning towels, and pass around the warm-up bottles of *Dr. McGilligudy's Peppermint Schnapps* and *Absolut Vodka* and *Boone's Farm* screw-cap wine.

All the energy in the place turns to what is coming. They hand the bottles around and pound it back as they rush through the required maintenance checklists from the Ministry of Public Health: Decks hosed and squeegeed, metal mirrors windexed, tests for chlorine and pH levels, eyedroppers dripped five times into tiny graduated cylinders. Spritzes of

WHMIS-approved disinfectant squirted into the urine-soaked corners of the bathroom stalls, toilet paper dispensers refilled, rodent-sized nests of woven anonymous hair scooped from the filter traps. Robot vacuum cleaners tossed into the deep end and dispatched for a night's work crawling along the bottom to consume lost Band-Aids, random coins, and flakes of discarded human skin.

Then out for some quick food, nachos or pizza, a cross-border run to Mexican Village. Pitchers of draft. More shots, ordered by the round and served in little plastic one-ounce glasses. *Sex on the beach* for the girls. Macho burning *Prairie Fires* for the guys. A bush party in the woods somewhere behind Holy Names High School or tents set up in a circle at Holiday Beach. Maybe Karaoke. Or taking advantage of the Tuesday night dollar-drink special at Club Vertigo. Shaking in the strobe lights, flashing in and out, writhing against each other until they turn on the real lights and the bouncers in their black STAFF T-shirts kick everybody out. A cooler waiting in the trunk of somebody's car. People pairing off and disappearing behind the warehouses. Gossip gearing up for the next day.

Somebody says, "Don't know about the rest of you, but I'm going over the side."

Talk about who is in and who is out. A dangerous, weaving, over-crowded, curb-scratching drive down to the river. The darkened side fire escape that goes all the way to the top. Guys do it in their boxers or fly off the side completely naked, but girls usually wriggle back into their blue, still-soaked suits. They arch their backs and mutter as they shimmy back and forth on the vinyl back seat or try unsteadily to step into the half-open leg holes while they brace themselves, not at all hidden, against the branches of a thin landscaping tree tied to a metal pole with a twist of wire and plastic. The nylon in the suits is so cold and sticky it makes all the tiny hairs on your arms and legs pop to attention and for the first fifteen minutes, before going over the side makes everything else secondary, the girls poke their thumbs in and pull against the seams around their armpits and hips because a wet swimsuit sucks out the air and clings so tight you may as well not be wearing one.

STACE SAYS, "I don't know about this."

She feels in-between. As though she is standing inside one version of herself while the next person in line, the girl she is about to become, gestures from a slight distance ahead and waits.

"Don't worry," Mel repeats. "Once you do it, it's done. Look."

She juts her chin in the direction of the other girl standing casually by the edge talking to the guys.

"Look. Even Krista's done it twice."

Stace looks and it is true. Even Krista. Twice.

Then Mel does one more thing. She reaches out with her open hand and places it in the centre of Stace's back, right at the intersection where the suit straps crisscross below her shoulders. She pushes her. It is only a nudge.

"Out of the way," Mel yells. "Coming through."

Everyone turns and Brad is there, dripping in his boxer shorts and smiling. Like the rest of them, like most of the Lifeguards, like every serious swimmer, he seems purposely designed for water. He has long arms that hang down to his knees, big hands and big feet. There is a slightly green tinge in his hair and if he stays out of the pool too long, he starts to look flaky and overly dry. The team he is on practices early in the morning and again in the afternoon, four hours a day. He is capable of almost anything. Stace has watched him sit cross-legged on the bottom of the deep end, holding his breath for five minutes, without any sign of struggle. There's a tattoo of the Canadian flag on his shoulder, an earring glinting on the left side of his head, and the stubble on his chest and legs is just beginning to grow back.

The red light reflecting from the big O in the Odeon sign shines up on one half of him and from this angle Stace thinks he barely seems possible. He is not a real person anymore, but something more like a photo-shopped image of what *the* person is supposed to look like – Victor Davis at the Olympics – or the template Lifeguard character cut from the Sears Catalogue and brought to life with all his altered pixels and re-touchings. It seems like his whole torso, the bones of his rib cage and the internal organs that beat and pulsate inside of him, have been packaged like this to accentuate the way those two S-shaped slivers of muscle run lean down his sides before cutting across his abdomen and swerving – it's ridiculous – swerving like two arrows leading your eyes down the front of his shorts. The wind continues to move over and around everybody else, but he does not shiver. He is, like her, somewhere in his early twenties, but Stace senses that his time is already passing. At the very most, he can keep it up, stay impossible like this, for only two or three more years.

An hour ago they were dancing in the blinking lights at Vertigo. She turned her back to him, bent her knees and leaned her shoulders into his chest. She let him rest his hands on her hips and run them down over her thighs in time to the throbbing music. They swayed like that, both facing the same direction and sometimes she would reach all the way around and put her hand on his back to pull him in closer and feel his whole body coming through his clothes. Sweat dripping down from his hair and the tip of his nose, his sternum square and flat in the middle of his chest, and his already hard cock, bent sideways in his jeans. He put his fingers on the side of her face, pulled the hair away from her ear and half-kissed her neck. Though the music was loud and she could feel the beat coming up through the floor, she heard it clearly when he whispered about how he had always wanted her.

"Always," he said. "Since that first day, right from the beginning. I knew we would end up like this. I could feel it from the start."

"Me, too," she told him, not turning around. "Me, too."

FOR THE LAST SEVERAL MINUTES – since they spilled out of the car and climbed to the roof – she had been trying to figure out exactly where they stand now relative to each other. She sat on his lap in the car and he put his hand on the bare skin of her stomach, in the gap between her T-shirt and jeans. On the roof, they snatched quick secret looks back and forth. In the complicated calculus of getting it on, she knows they are approaching a limit, but she isn't sure what the line signifies, or what a step across it will require.

A slow clapping starts up and she hears her name chanted, broken down into two halves.

– *Stay-see*, the voices say.

Then again – *Stay-see* and *Stay-see* and *Stay-see*.

When the speed picks up and the clapping gets faster, the back becomes the front and all she hears is – *see-Stay*, *see-Stay*, *see-Stay*. Brad's voice rumbling through under the other sounds. There is something extra in the way he calls her name.

The added attention makes it impossible to do nothing anymore. She starts up: left, right, left, right, in time with the rhythm. *Stay-see*, *Stay-see*, before *see-Stay*, *see-Stay*. Her arms follow along, pumping, and her breath goes in and out, a bit ragged. With every rotation she is running out of space. When she plants down hard for the takeoff, she splashes into the middle of a small puddle that has formed in the jumping-off spot others have already used many times before. Even as she tries to launch herself out, she feels the slip, all her traction giving out. She knows it immediately, knows with an absolute and instant clarity, that she doesn't have enough. There is no force behind her, no momentum to carry her forward. As she goes over the side, stumbles really, she hears Krista's tinny, whiny voice and catches the two, sucked-in, hissing words.

– "Missed it."

There is nothing in the sky. A thin whispering dark surrounds her while another one, a different dark, thicker and shifting, waits below.

As she falls, she is surprised to find that even as it is happening – even as her voice pours out and her arms and legs wheel in the air and she rolls down so clumsily and so totally unlike a swan – even as this is happening, she is surprised to find there is time for lucid reflection and simple calculations. How did she get here, to exactly this point? What purposeful first step could have lead so directly to that last one?

There is also enough time to think about the way something soft passes through something hard. Cheese yielding to the cheese grater. Playdough's Fuzzy Pumper Barber Shop. The garlic press. Greasy burgers dripping on the grill. The carts are a hard net waiting below the high wire act, a sieve.

All the way out, then all the way down.

She thinks about her arc, her way through the air.

How far is far enough? How close too close? Her cheeks inflate, a pair of useless parachutes. The light in the water or the light in the sky turns sideways and the Renaissance Center seems to bend over and touch its toes. She tucks her eyes into the crook of her elbow, braces against the emptiness, and waits for contact.

*

Before any of this, the ocean came first. It was the original problem and if you had to look for beginnings the source for everything that came later. She was seven years old, travelling with her parents on a doomed vacation in Nova Scotia and it happened on a sharp, stony beach across the highway from a cluster of brown housekeeping cottages. Each little plywood house had a clever kitchenette, a folding table, two sets of bunk beds, green polyester comforters and a supply of thin, over-laundered towels. The cupboards held place settings for four and came equipped with nearly enough cutlery. A regular tourist place, nothing special, but it comes back to her all the time, like a crime scene photograph, barging uninvited into her mind with all its black and white details. Before she took hold, signed herself up and started to turn around, almost anything could trigger an attack.

There was – she remembers – a time a couple of years ago when a visiting license plate from 'Canada's Ocean Playground' went into her brain the wrong way and her throat started to close up all on its own. Her neck felt like an arm squeezed inside a blood-pressure cuff. She started to cough and gagged and had to turn away from the street, sit down on a park bench, close her eyes, and put her head between her knees. She cupped her hands over her mouth and nose and concentrated hard on sucking back her own air until the sleeve loosened and the clenching hissed away.

It had become a biological fact in her life, like a severe allergy or a fundamental and unalterable weakness in her body. Bad news stamped out in her genetic code. Fear was an illness, a virus that forced its way in, compromised your immunity and damaged your defences in ways that couldn't be fixed. There was a force that lived inside of all deep water – she knew it intimately – a starving, swallowing power that pulled everything down into itself. It had chased her for years, back from Nova Scotia, away from the pool parties of her childhood and the reckless Spring Break opportunities of high school and university. Even long bridge crossings made her uncomfortable and she never liked it when the airplane stewardesses, with their bored and glassy expressions, pretended to pull the tabs that would inflate the lifejacket under your seat in the unlikely event of an emergency. And those trickling sounds – the recordings of breaking waves some people used for relaxation – they gave her a twisting feeling deep in her gut and bowels, as if someone were wringing out her intestines like a wet dishcloth.

She'd seen something like it only once before in another person, a woman in an elevator. There was no predicting it. The doors closed like they always do and the little room started its descent. But then the woman's eyes went erratic and she made a whimpering sound and involuntary muscle spasms rippled up through her back and shoulders and neck.

She said it quietly first, "I have to get out of here. I have to get out right now." Then louder: "Let me out. Let me out. Open the door. I have to get out."

She pounded on the red emergency button and her head swivelled around the top and bottom corners of the elevator, looking for a different exit. Then there was an exhausted groan, a full submission, and she went blank and fainted. Stace caught her by the waist as she went down and when the doors opened on the ground floor she was holding this stranger's body up. The lady's head rested on her shoulder like a sleeping toddler.

NOVA SCOTIA HAD BEEN wrong from the start and they should have turned back earlier. It rained for a week, seven solid days and nights. The wipers got stuck at their highest setting and even when the sun came out, they kept banging back and forth like a pair of deranged metronomes. Her father missed the turn at Rivière-du-Loup, couldn't ask for directions, and had to double back. Nothing was where it was supposed to be. The Bluenose Schooner from the dime was out on tour and a lazy-looking moose nearly killed them when it wandered out of the fog on the Cabot Trail. They swerved to avoid her and the guard rail left a long scar across their sliding door on the passenger side. Stace broke a tooth at the Fortress of Louisburg biting into an unbuttered chunk of old-fashioned, "historically accurate" bread that looked like a cannon ball baked in a dusty forge. They drank only Pepsi and ate nothing but blond, deep-fried morsels of indistinguishable seafood served in fake woven baskets with red and white checked wax paper and little plastic cups of pale green coleslaw served on the side. When the rain finally gave up, the air still felt damp and cold.

Her mother saw an opening in that first patch of sunlight.

"This is it," she said. "Today we are going swimming. Come on. At least once before we go back. I want Stacey to feel what it's like, the real ocean."

Her father tried to shut it down.

"I don't know," he said. "Look at it."

Across the road, the water steamed in steady and grey and metallic, like an assembly line churning through its rotations. Before they broke, the waves rose up three or four feet, not big, but jagged-looking and ugly. You could see chunks of debris and streaks of roiled-up seaweed in their faces like lines of graffiti scrawled on broken concrete walls.

"I think we better leave it alone this time," he said. "Nothing we can do."

He had a cold coming on. Stace could see red veins cracking in the corner of his eyes.

"Maybe we can lay low today. Go for a walk, pick some shells, take some pictures. Get something good to eat. We'll book real lessons when we get back."

"No," her mother said, pushing it all the way through. "When are we going to get the chance again? A girl can't go through life being afraid of a little cold water."

He didn't have the strength.

"Whatever you want," he said and he held up both his hands so she could see all ten of his fingers.

"But this one is all yours. I'm not going in."

THE BEACH MADE STACE think of a city park during a garbage strike. To find a spot for their towels, they stepped through a jumble of sharp rocks, faded blue bottles of fabric softener and shredded Styrofoam buoys. There were a couple of broken lobster traps with short brown nails sticking out through the lathe and some larger, irregular shaped logs, even whole trees, bleached a petrified white, like the leftover bones of a rotted sea monster. Long, unfollowable lines of yellow rope wove in and out of the boulders and there were dozens of smashed Alexander Keith's beer bottles scattered around a firepit. At the far corner of the beach, at the base of the cliff, Stace found a kid's inflatable raft with paddles and oar locks and everything. It was a faded pink and yellow colour and there was a picture of a surfing Barbie on the punctured plastic floor.

WHEN STACE PUT HER FOOT in the ocean for the first time, the water came on hot, scorching hot and not cold at all. It seemed to pour itself into the space where her ankle met her shin and it felt like a metal crowbar had been jammed into her weakest soft spot and was trying to pry her open.

Her father came to watch but he wore his jeans and a heavy sweatshirt as a sign of protest. He sat on an overturned milk crate and opened his book.

"I am here as a witness," he told them. "You wouldn't catch me dead in there."

It was hopeless. Three minutes in needed twenty minutes out. Five minutes required half an hour. Between trips, they wrapped themselves in layers of summer-coloured towels, hopped on the spot and took turns drinking hot chocolate from a thermos. They never went in past their hips. Below the surface, the beach sloped away from the shore at a sharp angle and after five or six steps, dropped away completely.

"You need to relax," her mother repeated. She squeezed her hands too hard against Stace's cheeks and spit instructions into her bluing ear.

"Belly up," she said.

"Belly up. Lean all the way back. Look at the sky. Look at the sky."

There was no chance. The cold came all the way through, making it impossible to sense anything else and whenever Stace felt even the beginnings of a fragile balance, a new wave would barge through and wash out her best efforts. The terrible salt water went fiery up her nose, into her eyes and down her throat. When she rolled onto her front, she put her hands on her mother's shoulders and tried to blow bubbles and kick.

"Great, great," her mother said.

"That's the way. You're doing well."

It happened maybe a minute before they would have given up on their own. The big wave, the one that did it, seemed sent on purpose, an extra pulse of energy whipped into the sheet of water a hundred miles offshore and timed exactly for this task, triple the size of the ones immediately before and after. Her mother faced the shore and Stace was on her back again, looking up and hoping this would be the last time. The wall of water came into her vision, looming over her mother's shoulder like an old-style gangster thug sifting out of the crowd in a grey trench coat with the brim of his fedora pulled down low. He was so thick and so wide, he blocked out the sky. He shoved her mother forward headfirst into the sand before grabbing the girl and carrying her off in the opposite direction.

Stace felt each one of her mother's fingers releasing from around her head before the water spun her sideways and drew her away. She tried to thrash against the current and get her head back to the surface, but in the gritty mess she lost all sense of direction and couldn't tell if she was moving up or down. They called this an 'undertow.' That was the word to describe what was happening. People said to watch out for it and she'd seen the letters printed out on warning signs. *Use Caution: Severe Undertow. Beware: Dangerous Undertow in this Area.* She thought the name was exactly right: an explanation that must have come from someone who felt this once and was able to report back to other people. Undertow. Water, working like a rope, like a tangled line attached to a massive winch at the bottom. I am going down the drain, she thought. I am going down.

The ocean was vast and empty and it could move in several different directions at the same time. It jostled her and she felt her neck snap back very hard while her hips and her legs went the other way. She reached out her arms, but there was nothing to hold onto and she felt like a person fumbling for the light switch in the middle of a dark room with a high ceiling and walls moving always farther apart. It could go on forever. She knew this. The ocean could go on forever.

Timing blurred. It was impossible to keep track of the minutes and seconds. The first flash of panic gave way to a cloudy, sleepy feeling. Nothing came in or went out – no air and no water. She felt completely full, as if all the gaps and extra spaces in her body had been made solid. She went limp and for a moment she felt like a floating thing, like a person who really might be able to move easily, and for a long time, in tune with the up and down beat of the ocean. This, she thought, this was it. Swimming. Almost right.

But then a series of sharp stinging pains came through her skull and she felt first the individual hairs, then whole clumps of her scalp being yanked out of her head. In a dizzy haze she thought she saw her father, but his glasses were gone and his sweatshirt seemed bloated and pulled strangely across his shoulders. His nose was scrunched up like something smelled very bad and he seemed angry, furious with somebody. She thought she heard her name.

"Stay with me Stacey," he said.

"Stay here. I've got you. It's going to be okay. We have you now. Stay with me."

When her face broke the surface, he let go of her hair, flipped her over and looped his elbow under her chin in a kind of reverse headlock that kept her mouth and nose above the water. The air felt thin and unsubstantial. He went under several times trying to side-stroke back to the shore, sometimes bounding off the bottom. When he could finally touch, he put her over his shoulder and carried her for the last few steps before dumping her back onto the beach like a leaking bag of garbage. He collapsed on his hands and knees and a thin mix of bloody snot and vomit poured out of him. She coughed up mouthful after mouthful of perfectly clear water, then rolled over and stuck out her tongue to taste the sand. It coated her face and the inside of her cheeks and she mashed the grit into her teeth.

Her mother put towels around the two of them and rubbed the girl's back, trying to get her to sit up.

"Can you hear me Stacey?" she said. "Are you okay?"

There was a raw trill in her voice and she placed her hands again on Stace's cheeks, steadied the head and tried to look into her daughter's eyes to see if there was anything there. She wasn't sure if the girl was actually coming back, was even conscious, or could stay that way.

"Are you all right, Stacey?" She was screaming it now, repeating.

"Talk to me. Say something. Can you hear me?"

Stace's head lolled off to the side and her eyes rolled back and showed her mother only whiteness. A sandy drool seeped onto her shoulder and she couldn't keep her mouth closed.

Her mother thought of paralysis and oxygen deprivation and permanent brain damage. There was a thing called secondary drowning. She'd read about it. A person could look like they'd been saved but still end up lost. You could be pulled living from the water and die three hours later with your head on your pillow and your lungs full of fluid.

"Stacey," she yelled. "Can you hear me? Tell me you're all right. Nod if you can hear my voice. Tell me you're okay. Look at me. Are you okay?"

The last thing the girl remembers is reaching out with her left hand and placing it over her mother's mouth. Then she sucked in one more breath and used that air to say the word "No."

*

She sees the water coming and then she doesn't. The river rolls in and out of her vision as she falls. She is halfway around, on her side, when she hits and the surface stings hot against her skin like an open-palmed slap extending from her cheek all the way down to her left pinkie toe. Spread out across the top, the impact knocks the wind out of her and for a second, while everything is distorted, she thinks maybe she has ruptured an ear drum and tastes a trace of blood spilling into her mouth. The fall is so awkward she barely sinks and instead burps back to the surface. She pulls in one clear gulp of air, and though she can't feel anything, not the temperature of the water or the air, she knows she is nearly perfectly unhurt. She forces her mind all the way down her arms and legs and makes her fingers and toes wiggle on command. She concentrates and tries to look below, but the dark and the silt obscure everything beyond her knees. When she extends her big toe and tries to feel around with her feet, she registers only an emptiness that might continue all the way to the bottom or might end in a wall of metal six inches farther down. As far as she can tell, the only hardness is the water itself and there is nothing else, no trap, waiting underneath.

She looks up at the hotel bedrooms, shakes her head, and wonders if any insomniac business travellers or romantic getaway couples caught a glimpse as she plummeted past their windows. The water really does taste like nothing and for a moment, as a warm exalted sense of relief washes all the way through her system, the current seems to be pushing her back to the side, back to the pilings and guiding her over to the good climbing out spot where there are two solid footholds and a bit of rope hanging down. Her ears are still foggy so she doesn't hear and doesn't respond to the worried calls from above. The mist casts a shadow over everything. They can't see her and she can't see them.

She is almost all the way back, almost out, the rope nearly in her hand, when she looks up at the M-shaped string of white lights hanging on the Ambassador Bridge like understated Christmas decorations. There is a faded image of the old Boblo boat, the Mississippi Paddler, painted on the side of a warehouse and permanent fires burning on Zug Island. The smokestacks leak unnatural combinations of purple and grey and almost pink.

She thinks about that man, the guy who jumped off the bridge several years ago in a failed suicide attempt. It was in the papers for weeks but it took a long time before the real story, the scandal, came out. They say he tried to kill himself but accidentally survived. That was the official version. Other people believed it was faked from the beginning. Even though dozens of witnesses had seen him jump, they still thought there had to be a trick behind it, some David Copperfield illusion.

Before tonight, Stace had never given one second of her time to this guy or his story. He was less than a fragment, a particle floating in her memory, one of the million unconnected facts you hear about and can't forget. Before tonight, she didn't know what to believe. Now, though, everything seems different and there is no confusion. She knows the fall could not have been planned or staged. Not from the bridge. Look at it. Not from that height. You couldn't try to survive something like that; you just lived through it. A fluke occurrence.

It must have been strange. He'd have been hurt for sure, broken bones and internal bleeding and the rest, but it must have been shocking to be awake and completely aware of what was happening. The guy on the bridge, he wanted everything to stop when he reached the river. He was hoping to hit on a real ending, but then – surprise, surprise – all these new choices, the nasty ones, showed up only after he found himself floating on his back and he could still breathe and still see out through his eyes.

That's probably when it came to him, she thinks, while he was moving in the current and looking at the sky.

Police on both sides of the border looked for his body for weeks. They dredged the river and sent dogs sniffing along the shore. When nothing turned up, the family believed he was lost for good. There was a funeral and a little insurance money. They went on and lived without him for years, building up entirely new versions of themselves. The kids moved away and the wife met somebody else.

Then the postcards started to arrive from some messed-up version of heaven. Miami, maybe, or The Magic Kingdom. The handwriting was unmistakable and the postmarks were recent. He wrote about how he missed them and loved them very much. He said he didn't want them to worry anymore.

STACE BRINGS HER ARM out of the water, circles it through the air, and cuts back in. It feels almost like the beginning and she is surprised by the relaxed, instinctive slice of her hand moving through. Her body can do something it couldn't do before. She looks at her fingers, barely visible beneath the surface and has to remind herself of what is happening. She is swimming at night by herself in the Detroit River. On the other side, the windows and elevators of the Renaissance Center shine like a downtown lighthouse only a mile away. In the pure terms of distance, it is not that far. One mile. In the pool, the whole expanse would be cut into 64 equal lengths and she does that almost every other day. If she really wanted to, Stace could swim to America, all the way to Hart Plaza. She could pull herself out, climb over the little fence, walk into the middle of the city and stand there in her dripping bathing suit, right in front of the statue of Joe Louis's big hanging fist.

She thinks about the decisions people make about themselves, the man on the bridge, gains and losses. It has been almost a year, but it still feels strange, sometimes even disturbing and wrong. Water cannot hold her anymore. She enters and leaves as she pleases. Climbs out and dives back in. When she moves through the river, she sculpts it around her body, makes it go exactly where she wants. The sting is fading and she is almost back to the side, getting ready to pull herself out, when she sees it: the pale outline of a human body streaking out of the sky like a hero from Greek myth. Like an actual guardian, a protector of life. He is a lightning bolt fired from the top of a building and he is purposely aimed, she can see it in the way he flies, aimed for her rescue.

*

"This is how it is supposed to be. Don't you feel it? We've been on our way to this since the very beginning. Like a collision."

They were on the floor at Vertigo, dancing in the strobe light, flashing in and out, a series of still photographs.

"I know," she said.

"You remember the first day? When you were tossed in there with everybody else? I didn't know what to do. Couldn't figure you out."

"Yes," she said. "I remember it. Of course I do. But it was different for me. You wouldn't understand. You couldn't."

THE FIRST CLASS was the second Tuesday after Labour Day. He checked her name off his clipboard list and she felt the way his eyes slid up and then down over the tight black contours of her new suit. It had been there from the beginning.

"You sure you're in the right place?" he asked.

She wanted to keep it light. That had always been the plan. Treat it like nothing and get through.

"Think so," she said. "I mean this is the first level, right? Adult Beginner I?"

She showed him the receipt.

"See? Seven-thirty to eight-fifteen. The Rec-Guide says this is the place to start. The place for people who don't swim at all. The first class. For people who don't go in over their heads."

His eyes wavered and he shook his hand like he needed her to stop talking.

"My fault," he said. "Sorry. My fault. Adult Beginner I. Yes. Right place. Totally fine. No problem. My mistake."

He told her later, weeks afterward, when everything was different, that she didn't look right. Not like one of his normal students. The others in the class were older ladies, senior citizens taking advantage of their discounts. Some were regulars, back for their fourth or fifth session with Brad.

"He's the absolute best." A lady with a thick blue bathing cap embossed with flowers told her that early on.

"So patient and so kind and so nice. He tries to make it fun for us."

The women in the class were the other kind of elderly. Spunky, silver-haired adventurers. Takers of tango lessons and passengers on European tour buses. They wore waterproof makeup in the pool and their bathing suits came in the cruise colours – citrus yellow and orange and lime green –

119

with tropical prints of toucans and palm trees and extra frilly layers of fabric stitched around the middle.

Brad's every movement sent vibrations through their bodies. Whenever he dove in or pulled himself back onto the deck – picture a slick performing dolphin at Marineland – the girls gasped and turned to each other, bubbling and giggling. Stace could imagine them sixty-five years ago, in braids and pig tails, passing folded notes at the back of a one-room school house.

They would do anything he asked. Whenever he called or waved his hands, another one pushed away from the side and went lustily flopping out to join him in the middle of the deep end. Stace didn't like these women. She thought they lacked solid convictions and reliable stick-to-itiveness. They gave up without struggle or protest and they hurried for improvement, rushing to fix up all their old deficiencies and sacrifice their fears to this boy in his Speedo.

Brad made them practice a manoeuvre he called *The Blast Off.* Or sometimes *The Rocket Ship.* You had to reach back with your arms locked straight at the elbow and face out into the middle of the diving well. With your fingers clawed into the gutter, you leaned all the way forward, submerged up to your neck. Your chin rested on the surface, your legs coiled, and your feet pushed flat against the vertical tile of the pool wall. All the tension in your body strained forward, preparing for ignition. It was horrible. Whenever he got Stace into that position, she felt trapped by her own contorted limbs, folded-up, like a person in a straightjacket. An uncomfortable pressure seeped through her insides, a near-bursting feeling, like the desperate urge to pee.

The ladies tried their best, tried to do it right, tried to look as if underneath the jokes and silly pretending, they really could swim any time they wanted. They wanted to

Blast Off and join Brad in the middle of the deep end, but it never worked like that. Instead, as soon as they released, as soon as they let go, their smiles flattened and their bodies hardened. They failed so completely, so quickly and perfectly, that Brad sometimes had to flash over and dive down or sink his hand way below his knees to get hold of an armpit or a flailing hand or the corner of a bathing suit. When he brought them back to the surface, the women broke to the air spitting and sputtering and sometimes they let out these huge pressurized belches that sounded like they came from deep in their stomachs. He'd cover up the uglier sounds with encouragement and say things like, "That was a good try, Gladys," or "No problems here. We're getting closer every day."

When they tried to share in his optimism, tried to smile back into Brad's face, that was true conversation, the kind of perfect communication Stace could understand. The way it all returned: old terrors carving themselves back into the familiar creases around their eyes. The deep end was like a reversed fountain of youth. Confident ladies full of laughs went out and went under, but the people who came back were thin-haired and fragile. The people who came back were panicked and stiff and confused and not sure of anything anymore. Lines of mascara ran down their faces and the whitest of the bathing suits went all the way over to transparent, revealing knots of pubic hair and leaving nothing to the imagination anymore. The women sobbed sometimes and cried out. They dug their fingernails into Brad's neck and shoulders. Stace could see a fresh constellation of half-moons and purplish crescents cut out of his skin, layered over older scars.

She resisted him for the first four weeks and always passed when it was her turn to Blast Off. She felt no attraction when his eyes locked on hers and she did not want to be in the same place with him.

"Come out to me," he said.

"It's not far. Just breathe and relax and let yourself go. It's easy, easy, easy. Let it go. Come on. Out to me. Right now. Come on."

His hand reached over to her with the palm up, but he kept the tips of his fingers just out of range. He could stay like that for hours, dropped in the middle, with both hands and half his chest out of the water, relaxed and conversational, like he was standing on the top rung of a glass ladder that went all the way to the bottom.

But she could see the strategy. As soon as she trusted and let go, he'd move backwards, slither away and leave her out there by herself.

"It's all in your head," he said. "That's where it starts and where it ends. Trust me. Come on. Now. Come out to me right now."

There was a catch in his voice sometimes. A small hesitation, like he was holding back on a secret he couldn't tell them yet. This was his job, work he got paid to do, and there were moments, she could see them, moments when he really had to try hard to keep his true feelings down. How many times in a week did he end up like this? How much waiting and coaxing and lying were required to get through an average Tuesday night? The worn out pick-up lines of the swimming teacher: how many times did he have to burn through them?

"You need to trust and let go. I'm right here. Come on."

Sometimes while he waited he would fire a narrow squirt-gun stream of water through the small gap in his front teeth.

By the fifth week, the other ladies had had enough.

"Don't be such a suck," the woman beside her said. She waved her hand out to the middle.

"No need to make a big show. Just go for Godsakes."

"I can't," Stace said. "I'm not ready. Still have to sort some things out. I'm working on it."

She hated even trying to talk about it. What words could you use? How would you describe this feeling? She tried to smile.

"We'll see. Maybe next week. We'll see. But you guys are doing great. I learn a lot by watching."

The woman laughed in her face.

"You're working on it?" she said. The maternal scolding in her voice was impossible to cover up.

"Learning. Maybe next week. Can you hear yourself talking? Look around. Look at yourself. What in the world do you have to worry about? You'll make it. Just go. Go."

Brad took his cue.

"She's right," he said. "Take your turn. Can't keep dodging. I'm right here."

FOR A MOMENT, she could imagine it: letting go and pushing away, flying toward Brad. She wanted to be chosen and she believed there must be something like a transparent hand that lived inside of water. It made permanent selections and cradled some people, holding them always at the top, but it dragged other people down to the bottom and there was no way to protest.

"What you need to do is get over yourself," the lady said.

"I'm getting sick of you sitting there watching the rest of us drown."

She sneered and reached over to grab Stace's right hand. She pried the girl's fingers off the gutter and flung her whole arm out into the water.

"Go on," she said.

Stace watched her hand splash down hard in front of her face. Brad took it, gave a sharp tug and pulled her away completely.

"Come," he said. "This is it."

A hot pulse of anger passed through her.

"Wait," she said. "Wait."

But it couldn't be stopped. The hand triggered a chain reaction – the slowest Blast Off in history – and she felt the spring uncoiling, her arms, legs, torso and neck letting go. Brad backed away immediately and moved way out to the centre.

A single perfectly clear breath entered her body and for about five seconds everything was exactly as it should be. She went horizontal, parallel to the ceiling and floor, her weight spread out across the surface tension of the water. She even propelled herself forward, kicking. Her hands scooped through a dog-paddle and she inched towards Brad and his retreating hand.

"Good, good, good," he said. "Out to me. Come on. You've got it now."

He smiled. He smiled for her, but kept backing away.

"Look at you," the lady called out, genuinely happy.

"I told you so. You're doing it. You're doing it right now."

*

When Brad comes to her in the river, when he crosses over and reaches out, it will feel like swimming with no clothes, like skinny-dipping. His body – cold and slippery and hard – will press tight against hers and the water, moving all around and below, will push them wherever it wants. He will get it, understand immediately, and feel what she feels right now: stupid and spared. The same tingling, an electric charge of appreciation for what might have been lost will zip through his system. When they touch for the first time down here, deep where no one else can see, she will initiate the contact and make her intentions clear. Her already wet tongue, still salty with the diluting hint of blood, will go into his mouth and slide around and she will reach down between his legs without hesitating. He will know what to do. When they climb out, the required excuses will be made and they will leave the others behind. Maybe it will happen at his apartment, on a futon mattress on the floor, or maybe in a tent, maybe on the beach with the waves lapping at their toes, any dark place he wants, a car, it doesn't matter, but it will happen tonight, as soon as possible.

She holds the rope and waits. The current sways her like a kid on a tire swing and she can imagine the time unfolding. In a couple of seconds, his head will break through the surface and he will pop up like a curious seal. At first, he will wear one of those urgent, serious and worried expressions. His mind will be crowded with procedures: the right roll-over for a floating spinal injury, what to do if he finds her unconscious and face-down.

But when she waves and calls out, when he hears her voice, sees her on the swing, it will change. The charge will flow and his worry will fade. He'll smile and anticipate and his arms will churn. He will crawl through the water, cutting the fastest, straightest line directly to her body.

She waits some more, a little longer, the smile still stretched on her face, but he doesn't come up. It seems darker than before and against the shifting backdrop of the water, it is hard to mark any clear distinctions or to see very far. An echo from the past, the sloshing of broken wave, whispers in her ear. Her shoulders tighten. Time builds on itself. She pulls herself up a little higher, concentrates, and tries to pick out the exact spot where he entered the river. She can retrace his path through the sky and she knows he came through bullet smooth. He went in deep, the way you practice it on the high dive, and left no splash, no ripples or wake to follow back to the centre of his entry. The wind gusts and she feels the first real chill pass though her body. Her hands are chaffing and with her adrenaline waning, she feels the first true ache begin to emerge from her body. An early redness spreads across her skin, the start of what will be the deep black and purple of an all-over bruise. It has been too long. Already way too long.

Where?

She tries to suppress the question. To think it through calmly. But there are limited possibilities. He is either coming towards her right now or he is not coming at all. Either he is swimming under the surface, playing submarine, already close by and ready to reach out and pinch her and laugh; or he is in bad shape somewhere else, quiet, and carried in the current of a dark river.

There is only one other option. He is not moving at all, not at the surface, not in the current. Limbs wedged between the bars of an underwater cage. Something soft passing through something hard. A picture from TV comes into her mind: One of those deep-sea camera crews, scuba divers with long poles standing in a metal box. They pour a mix of blood and fish guts and stir the chum, baiting the Great Whites to come closer.

She puts her face in the water and opens her eyes, but there is nothing to see. On the other side, she cranes her neck upward and tries to look over the edge of the roof. Nobody is left. Probably on the fire escape working their way to the ground, she thinks. Probably on their way. But that will take at least two minutes. Two more minutes.

She calls anyway, yelling the question up against the face of the building, the hotel windows, the Odeon sign.

"Do you see him?" she asks.

*

On the night she learned to swim, Stace had to go down before she could come back up. After the Blast Off, she moved toward Brad, but he kept pulling back until he was almost all the way over to the other side and she knew she would never reach him. There was progress at first. She stayed at the surface for what felt like a long time. But then her patience ran out and her concentration lurched. Her eyes wandered from the pruned fingers of his hand and went up to the ceiling, to the network of criss-crossing catwalks and lights and girders above her head. Her chin followed and tilted, and her shoulders dropped and her hips and legs and feet lowered a bit, and then a little bit more, until she was straight up and down, vertical and wrong, standing at attention in deep water. When the grip came back it reached out of the blackest part of her memory and closed around her ankle. It felt like a set of slender fingers, or a vine or some coiling tentacle, extending up from the bottom of a swamp. It pulled her down patiently, insistently, as if there were no need to rush. Her second breath came in a garbled mix of half-water, half-air and every muscle in her body contracted. She felt like she was rusting all the way through and she went down so fast that Brad could not get back in time to make his grab. She sank to the bottom like an object with no life in it, like a bronze sculpture of a swimmer, heaved overboard.

Below the surface, though, it was not what she expected. The underside of the swimming pool did not feel like the ocean. Not the same element, not water the way she remembered it to be. In the pool, all the valves and pipes that made the place possible – the pumps and filters and automated heating elements – sent out waves of precisely controlled sound. She exhaled through her nose as she descended and listened to the humming: a boring, competent drone, a *hmmmmmmmmmmm* that might go on forever, like the buzz of office lighting or the murmur that leaks from computers.

There was a trance, a hypnotic suggestion, inside that sound. She yielded to it and let herself be absorbed. It made her think of cubicles and automatic pencil sharpeners and taking a number from the dispenser to wait in line for your driver's license to be renewed.

That's when it happened. An understanding, a new realization, came into her head and triggered a transformation that was almost total. Maybe this was how all learning worked in the end. The right kind of concentration deployed in the right way at the right time. If you paid attention and sorted carefully, put things in the right place at the right time, it was possible to think yourself away from yourself, away from the things you could not do. Like a child bicycle rider who hits on that ancient balancing trick for the first time and races away from her parents, Stace felt herself changing, her capacities expanding. In one moment of insight, an action that once seemed mysterious and impossible entered the realm of the clear and knowable.

She saw it now: A swimming pool was more parking lot than ocean. Right angles, a perfect square with no secrets, utterly transparent, bleached. It was like a beaker in the lab, an ice cube tray under the tap. If you did not fear it, you could not be scared.

She rolled back through the advice she'd been given. It really was in your head. That was true. You had to relax, yes, and, no, you could not fight it. If you knew that going under, that submersion, was only a temporary condition and if you accepted that little bit of pressure, the water pushing back, then you could open your eyes and hold a breath without worrying about the next one. You could go to the bottom, feel the tiles under your toes and look up at other people's feet, other bodies floating above your head. See through to the light on the other side.

And if you truly figured it out – if you really understood a swimming pool – you could wait there on the bottom for a few calm seconds. You could shrug off years of wrong-headed pain and leave it on the floor like an overburdened backpack. You could Blast Off in reverse. Push up and away, fly back to the surface. Your life could be altered, changed forever, in less than ten seconds.

SHE PASSED BRAD on her way up and he missed her for the second time. When they surfaced, he was the one panting, obviously flustered and angry.

"What the hell was that?" he said. "Is this a joke? Were you trying to do that, go down as fast as you could?"

"No," she said. She smiled at him. "No."

She put one hand on the gutter and looked down, first at her feet scissoring back and forth in the waveless warm water, then lower, all the way to the bottom.

"Maybe you aren't ready for this," he said. "Maybe we need to go back to the shallow end and start again."

" No," she said again. "No." It came out crisp and fast.

"I'm sorry about all this," she said. "It was my fault. But it's okay now, I think. Let's pretend it never happened."

IT COULD NOT BE EXPLAINED. And it would have been impossible to lead another person down the strange corridors and passageways, the new-firing synapses of her brain. Brad had never seen anything like it: Water letting go. The film of worry cleared completely from somebody's eyes. A girl turning herself around so quickly.

She moved forward every week. First the floats and the introductory front swim. She could see them now, understand how everything fit together, the breathing and the basic movements flowing into each other. He made precise adjustments, guided her arms and legs with just the tips of his fingers, moved her head with an open palm on her cheek. The back swim and the kneeling front dive and the stride jump. She went down to the bottom and retrieved three or four rubber rings at a time. At the end of each class, they treaded water for thirty seconds longer. His head bobbed close to hers as he counted off the time and she could see droplets of water hanging in his eyelashes.

He gave her a copy of the Royal Life Saving Society manual. The book was a yellow and blue three-ring binder with the society's logo printed on the cover. An oar crossed with a grappling hook and knotted together with a shamrock of coiled rope. Everything you needed to know was in there: what to do with poison, electrocution, a severed finger in a glass of milk, plucked eyeballs. If you fell into sub-zero water you were supposed to float on your back with your knees curled up to your chest. This kept your dwindling body heat concentrated in the core area. It was called H.E.L.P. – the Heat Escape Lessening Position. A drowning victim would grasp at anything to survive and a rescuer would have to ensure personal safety before trying to aid another. If a victim pulled you down you were supposed to strike hard and move back immediately, kick to the face or stomach or groin if necessary.

And if they became hysterical or violent, you had to stand by, just out of reach, and wait until they lost consciousness before moving in to help.

She took everything in. At the end of the session Brad made her a construction paper report card and drew happy faces and stars beside all the skills she had completed. He gave her five coloured badges from the Red Cross Kids program.

"I guess you're in Green now," he laughed. "And not too far from a shiny Bronze Medallion if you keep it up."

The ladies were not impressed.

"He's not supposed to do that, you know," one of them said.

"Those badges are for children. He's not supposed to do that. I'm sure you have to pay extra for badges."

SHE LEFT THE CLASS after fourteen weeks and never came back for Advanced Beginner II. On the last day, Brad helped her fine-tune the front crawl.

"Keep your head down, face in," he told her. "When you breathe, you have to turn your head instead of lifting it. Like this. You have to move your head from side to side instead of up and down. Like you're saying a big 'No' instead of a 'Yes.'"

She incorporated the breathing into the efficient cycle of her stroke, her head turning just enough to raise the corner of her mouth out of the water. At Christmas, they offered a fifty-percent discount for students who signed up for a full-year membership. She got a card and started coming almost every day to practice her lengths. The accuracy of the place, she liked that most. One length, a trip to the opposite wall, was worth twenty-five metres and the return gave you fifty. The day always ended on a nice round number.

She did her best thinking after ten minutes, when she was warmed-up and hit on a good rhythm. Her senses blurred and she felt cut off and separate and alone. In the water, there was no taste or smell or feeling or sound. Only her vision stayed sharp and sometimes it seemed too clear. Through her no-fog goggles, she studied the black lane marker stretching along the bottom into an elongated capital "I."

400 meters: 16 lengths. 800 metres, a half mile, needed 32. When she was sure she could cover the whole mile, she asked her parents to come watch. They sat up in the observation deck for the whole forty-five minutes and when Stace climbed out – a little flushed maybe but not breathless – they clapped and waved. Her mother cried and wore an expression that seemed proud and happy, but also scared and confused at the same time.

They came down the stairs and her father gave her an awkward hug, pressing her wet body into the acrylic fuzz of his sweater.

"Whoa," he said. "Look at you go. Amazing."

Her mother shook her head. "I just don't know," she said. "Even as I'm watching you do it, I can't believe it's really you in there."

SOMETIMES, WHEN SHE PUSHED HARD, sawing back and forth between the walls, she thought about the person she used to be and wondered what had happened to that girl. She felt distant, like she had moved to rural China or to some other country where the climate, the language, the diet, religion, politics, architecture and culture were so completely foreign, so different, it made it hard to believe that your own past, the place you came from, could still exist somewhere else in the world. Where did you store them, your leftover superstitions and the ridiculous rituals that once guaranteed your safety? All the misplaced and abandoned beliefs: what did people do with them now? The

woman in the elevator, or the arachnophobes, and the para-
noids who felt sure they were being followed? What did they
do when they learned the truth? Where did they go? Who
did they become, how could they return?

She felt alone and stupid, embarrassed by the force of her
flawed convictions. Years of her life had been sacrificed. She
was a fool, taken in by a lie, duped. It made her so angry she
stopped once – in mid-stroke, halfway down the pool. She
shook her head, ripped off her goggles and treaded water for
a couple of seconds in the middle of her lane while she took
it all in. Preposterous Lifeguards in their tank tops. Brad trying to look so severe as he glared down from his highchair.
A thin slippery film of piss-warm water coating the entire
deck. Two other swimmers, ugly manatees, bloated and
awkward and slow, sloshing between their pontooned guide
ropes. The four multi-coloured hands of the timer's clock
circling around every fifteen seconds. A burning stench of
antibacterial soap and chlorine wafting up from every
surface.

It was too much. She said the word *Fuck* and slapped the
warm, flat surface with her open hand. Nothing came back.
Her fingers passed down through the transparency. She felt
ashamed and exposed, like the last kid who refuses to let go of
the tooth fairy until some brute in the schoolyard says: "It's
your parents, you retard. They put money under your pillow
and throw your teeth away."

ONE TUESDAY NIGHT, early in the summer, she arrived late
and could only get in twenty minutes before the session
ended. She'd barely started when they blew the long whistle
and everybody had to get out. As she headed for the changing
rooms, one of the Lifeguards, a girl with a 'Melanie' name
tag, waved in her direction and walked over.

"Listen," the girl whispered, and she looked around to make sure they were alone.

"Listen, the place is yours if you want it. Nobody cares. We're stuck here for another hour of clean-up so you can finish up and stay as long as you like. It doesn't matter to any of us. It's not like you need somebody to watch over you."

She spoke with a sarcastic slacker tone that assumed mutual understanding. As though these two shared an equal part in a wider conspiracy.

Stace waited for the others to leave and watched as the girl went around with her necklace of keys, locking all the doors from the inside. Then Melanie turned and fanned her hand out across the pool.

"It's all yours," she said. "Go nuts."

*

It is time to go. Stace releases the rope, pushes out into the water as hard as she can. Near the sides, in the shelter of the pilings, the current is almost still, but it picks up quickly as she moves outward and pulls her away in a long diagonal. She can barely breathe, but she calls out his name, forces her face in, swings her arms and kicks. Something vegetal and slimy brushes up against her thigh and lets go. Her stroke is short and tight and she feels heavy, already exhausted. It is hard to stay up and difficult to go on. Every thirty seconds she has to stop and lift her head, get her breathing back and look for bearings. She searches above and below and yells again. His name, the word Brad, sounds pitiful and small.

We are made most specifically by the things we cannot bear to do. She realizes it now, feels it in the powerful movement of this different water. The old discomforts coming home: a familiar tightening in her diaphragm, the intimate constriction of her larynx, sticky weight in her arms and legs, the scurrying in her brain. Fear is our most private possession. Heights and crowded buses, reptiles and strangers, hot and cold, the smell of burning wood, loud noises: they persist. Takeoffs and landings, abandonment, holes in the ground, wide-open spaces, horned insects, the dark, earthquakes, mirrors, clocks, wind, deep water: they stay with us, forever in the world. Even when we overcome, they remain, reminding us of past truths. There can be nothing in their absence, not even the smallest possibility of a significant action.

But there is light. She thinks she sees it. A paleness flashes up about sixty feet away and goes back down. The object bobs in the current and disappears.

"Come out to me," she hears him repeating in her memory. "It's not that far."

The light is positioned at the limit of her vision. Beyond that spot, full darkness comes down like a heavy velvet curtain and the shadows make it impossible to be sure of anything. She chases it, moving as fast as she can. The wind blows in circles and a tiny island of floating garbage shoots past. A hinged styrofoam container that once held a Big Mac smiles at her as it surges through the foreground, pushed downstream so quickly it disappears in seconds.

She thinks about the Great Lakes, a project she did in elementary school, all five of them carved out in blue plasticine on a painted piece of plywood. It had been tricky to get the shapes and the scale right, difficult to get Lake Huron to fit correctly around the green mitten of Michigan. Information printed on her notecards: One quarter of all the fresh water in the world flows through here. A chain of liquid coursing in the middle of the continent. It blasts over Niagara Falls, and spills into the St. Lawrence before it finally reaches for the ocean.

The paleness in the water moves downstream and she pursues. It could be anything. His hand held out, always the target, or maybe his overturned back, the fabric in his boxer shorts. The lights on both sides of the river go dim and she is too far out now, too low to see the Renaissance Center, the Holiday Inn, and the Odeon. In the middle of the shipping lane, the water moves with its full force, pulled by gravity, by the lean of the land underneath and by tides thousands of miles away. She is inside of it now.

Jacques Cousteau came to shoot a movie. He was the reason for their grade-school projects. The *Calypso* sailed right down the middle of the Detroit River and the whole school went down to Dieppe Gardens to watch it go by. Stace stood on the concrete bike path, far back from the railings. The boat seemed old and rickety and wasn't as big as she expected. His yellow helicopter, stuck on the back, seemed like a toy.

Everyone cheered and clapped as he passed, but Cousteau never came out on deck to wave back. Her teacher said nobody in the world knew more about life underwater than he did. They played a record and showed a film strip in the darkened classroom. Stace had to sit beside the projector and turn the knob to advance the pictures every time she heard a beep.

Beep: Cousteau, standing on the deck, skinny and old with brown teeth, wearing the same red toque all the time. Beep: Cousteau in his gear, the aqualung respirator in his mouth, ready to roll backwards over the side. She thought he seemed too fragile to be down there with the Swordfish and the Killer Whales, the Manta Rays and the Giant Squid. Beep: Cousteau on the Great Barrier Reef. There were colours she had never seen before, real-life creatures that couldn't be real.

"Everything you can see in this picture is alive," the teacher said, the shadow of her hand showed on the screen.

"Even the rock is living."

Beep: Cousteau swimming under an Iceberg in the Antarctic Ocean. He is suspended in a grey void, an astronaut wandering in deep space. His slow voice coming out of the record player. The accent. He says, "From birth, man carries the weight of gravity on his shoulders. He is bolted to the earth. But he has only to sink beneath the surface and he is free."

The teacher made them memorize it.

They gave Cousteau a key to the city of Detroit and thousands stood in Hart Plaza to welcome him. But when he gave his speech, he turned furious and angry. His face contorted with rage and he talked about acid rain and illegal dumping, cancerous tumours and contamination of the food chain. Blind fish with confused sex organs. Mutating species.

"Your river, it is sick," he said.

"When we try to film, it is only dying we see down there."

There is a living tension, a line running between what can be achieved and what we cannot do. The light, the paleness inside the water, there is no way for her to catch it. He is beyond reach, moving at a pace she cannot match. A sentence from the lifesaving manual: Before all else, the rescuer's first duty is the preservation of the self. She gives up, surrenders, and turns back to try for the side.

In the middle of the river, the first hint of its approach is more than enough. She feels the throbbing of the engine coming through the water and hears the sound, a massive grinding, like a creature gnawing at the earth's crust. It is not visible yet, still out there and indistinct, but it is coming and she knows there will be no way around.

A raw terror sears through and demands an equivalent ferocity. She thrashes against the current, driven now by primordial instinct, the need to escape and a raw demand coming from a place she does not know. Her feet and hands pummel the surface. She snarls for breath, moving faster, harder than ever before. She is getting away, maybe, but there is no way to be sure. Every limit is unknown before it is reached. Very soon the prow, two hundred feet high, will emerge from the fog and it will part this water like the gargantuan head of an axe cleaving through. They are the native creatures of this place and the river is their natural habitat. Only the largest pass at night to avoid the complications of smaller boats. The propeller will be the size of a two-story house and the twin off-loading cranes will fold back like the wings of a resting insect. It will be a Leviathan, three football fields long, rusting red hide stuffed with 5,000 tons of salt. The river boils in its wake, a froth even the ocean cannot match. She tries not to hear it, tries to keep it out of her head, but the mechanical roar will not be commanded. It rises out of the dark, advances over the water and swallows everything in its path.

The Loop

The trick to riding a bike in the snow is to stand up on the pedals and push down hard on the front wheel. You need to lean into it and get all your momentum going forward so you can plough through that six or eight inches of slush that piles up on the side of the road. It's not a skill you can master. No matter how many times you go through and no matter how hard you think about it, it never gets any easier. That skinny little wheel still can't get a better grip on the ice-covered street. I used to think riding in the snow was the worst part of the Musgrave job, but in the end I had different reasons for quitting.

When you fall, you want to try and go down on the right hand side. As soon as you feel your tire slipping and the whole back end of the Supercycle moving away on its own, that's when you need to grab the bars tight and swing everything way over to the right, towards the hard line of parked cars. It has to be to the right because if you go down on the left you end up splayed out in the middle of the road, right at the peak of drive-home traffic, and all you can do then is hope those nervous Southern Ontario drivers – the ones who never buy winter tires – still remember how to pump their brakes in just the right way and swerve around you, carving a smooth S curve in the snow just a couple inches from your head.

The one time I went down like that, on the left, the delivery bag ripped open when I hit the ground and everything spilled out onto the street. I got tangled up in the frame and the shoulder strap got wrapped around my elbow and the snow-choked chain came off the big ring and the small ring at the same time. All the little white prescription bags and the brown bottles and the vials with their Musgrave Pharmacy stickers tumbled out. All the other stuff went too: the candy, the tampons, the eight-pack of toilet paper, the denture cream, the jars of medicated ointment and the magazines wrapped in plastic or discreet brown paper. I looked like a soggy hospital piñata that had been walloped into submission. The wet snow kept coming down in fat, lazy flakes and horns were squawking all around me. A steady stream of road-ragers chugged by, each one taking his turn to yell at me about how I better stay on the sidewalk or get the hell out of the way. There was a moment just after I hit the ground, when my head was still down there close to the asphalt and I saw one of those pill vials with the childproof cap rolling away from me, across the yellow line in the middle of the road. I was down right at eye-level and I saw it close-up as this black steel-belted radial came rolling down on it. The plastic tube made a quiet splintery sound and for a half-second I thought I saw a couple of blue and yellow capsules springing up maybe six inches off the ground before they were crushed into the blacktop.

When I finally got myself put together again and made it back to the store, Marlene, one of the nice older ladies who worked at the front counter selling film and batteries and stamps, took me into the tight bathroom on the other side of the dispensary. I remember the way she screwed the cap off a new bottle of rubbing alcohol and how she defiantly ripped open a package of the most expensive antiseptic-treated bandages we sold.

"The bastard," she muttered to me, as if we were suddenly the same age and we both had been in our jobs too long.

"There's no place he wouldn't send you. Nowhere is too far. Just the thought of it. On a day like today. You're lucky you're still alive."

She kind of cooed over me and tried to be as gentle as she could.

"It's going to hurt, Allan," she said. "But what can you do?"

She pressed the alcohol swabs into the scraped red lines on my left shoulder and my left elbow. And there was a weird moment when I had to undo the top button of my jeans and pull down my zipper just a bit so I could reach the bad spot where my left hip had come down the hardest. Marlene turned away and closed her eyes. Then she reached back and held out the dripping gauze.

"That one you can do yourself."

We both laughed.

When we came out, Musgrave was waiting. He was wearing a lab coat with his name embroidered on the pocket flap and holding one of those special metal spatulas they use for counting pills and sliding them across the tray. He pointed the sharp end of the spatula at me, right at the bridge of my nose, and he asked me if I was sure, absolutely sure, that nothing had been left behind.

"Those medications are controlled substances, you know," Musgrave said. "And from the minute they leave this dispensary, you are the one responsible for making sure they get where they're supposed to go."

He stared down at me through his bifocals and kind of swayed, shifting his weight from one foot to the other. Depending on how I looked up into his glasses from the other side, I could make his eyes change shape just by moving my head up or down.

"You're certain you got everything?" he said.

It was obvious he was worried mostly about his labels, about all those stickers with his name on them.

I thought about the crushed capsules again, about the stuff that was already gone, stuck to a tire somewhere and still moving across the city.

"There's nothing left," I said. "I brought back everything I could."

*

The guy really should have paid me more. Musgrave was always sticking me into tight situations I had to squirm out of on my own. A couple of years earlier, some high-school kids tried to rob me as I cut across Benson schoolyard. They thought I was carrying harder stuff they could use or re-sell and they tore through the packages looking for anything with codeine in it, for a big bottle of Tylenol 3s, or Percocets, or something with lots of ephedrine for making Crystal Meth. Today, they'd have been after the OxyContin.

When all they got was the regular stuff – the antacids and nasal sprays and laxatives and those sheets of little beige felt pads that you're supposed to stick to the corns on your feet – they turned angry. One of them knocked me over and held me down while another one pulled off my shoes. Then they tied them together and took turns swinging them above their heads, trying to throw them up as high as they could. After five or six cracks at it, one of them finally got it right and the shoes ended up tangled around a telephone line twenty feet above the street. They laughed and thought it was just perfect and left me alone after that.

But the shoes stayed up there a long time. Whenever I passed under them – if I was out on my route again or just out walking around near my house – I'd look up and feel that little sting coming up through the bottom of my socks, the same sharp digging pressure you get if you ever have to push your bare foot down onto the serrated edge of a pedal.

The place isn't even there anymore. A few months after I left, Musgrave gave it up completely and the store flipped into a Vietnamese grocery with roasted yellow ducks hanging in the front window and bushel baskets of fruit I didn't recognize. I think he held on for as long as he could, but he knew. Like the rest of us, Musgrave understood he was stuck at the end of things. It was during that period when the whole city wanted to go in a new direction, directly away from us, and the papers kept saying that we needed to tear down the old buildings on Pitt Street and "re-vitalize" everything. By the time they opened the brand new Shoppers Drug Mart, it was pretty clear. The new pharmacy had big windows that went all the way around the building from the floor up to the ceiling and every week they printed up a different full-colour flyer with all their specials in it. Shoppers Drug Mart had a fleet of blue and white delivery trucks driven by a crew of middle-aged men in matching coats. The trucks had a computer-tracking system, like a courier company, and every customer had to sign their name on a little digital pad before the driver would hand over their bag. They made their own cheaper, generic brands of everything. Soap and shampoo and vitamins and eye drops and aspirin and toothbrushes. Everything they sold had the word "Life" written on it, spelled out in this red slanty font. Nobody could compete with that.

"We're a dying breed," Musgrave told me once as he flipped through their latest flyer and stared at those glossy magnified photographs of hair dye and antiseptic mouthwash.

"Pretty soon, it's going to be impossible. Impossible for anybody to make a go of it on their own."

*

I'm pretty sure the customers I delivered to didn't know anything about the trucks or the better prices at Shoppers Drug Mart. Musgrave sent me mainly to the quiet floors of rest homes – to Golden Gate and Whispering Pines – and then out to his special harem of shut-ins and old women who had outlived their husbands. The other half of his customers were lonely single guys who'd been injured at the plants and were off on long-term disability. I had that job for almost three years, up to the end of elementary school, and except for a couple crashes and near-misses it was all pretty routine. From Monday to Friday between 4:00 and 6:30 I raced back and forth across the city, dodging cars and swerving around sewer grates with my bag always hanging over my shoulder and the weight in it clunking against my knee every time my leg came around for another turn.

I made a different plan for every trip. Before I left the store, I plotted the route out in my head and thought of all the short cuts I could take. And when I made the loop, I imagined it like a big connect-the-dots picture where I had to draw the lines between every separate person. I'd drop the right medicine at each house and maybe pick-up the prescriptions that needed to be filled the next time around. Every stop was its own thing but I held them all together in my head and I kept the whole sequence in order. It's like that for any delivery job. There's one address and then another and you keep leaving and arriving, but in between there's nothing.

I think the guys on disability had it roughest. They weren't as old as the women I delivered to and they didn't have the glaucoma or the osteoporosis that used to wear down the ladies. Instead, most of the guys had been wrecked by those steady, grinding jobs they used to have at the plants before everything got ergonomic and automated. Some of the men were so twisted up with tendonitis they couldn't tie their own shoes and when they went to shake your hand all you got was this flaccid jumble of separate fingers that wouldn't squeeze together right. They had joint and muscle problems and arthritis that was way worse than it should have been in people their age. And their lower backs were so messed up they had to sleep on sheets of plywood or lay on the floor when they watched their sports at night and their American soaps during the day.

Those kinds of injuries came from working on the line. They showed up in people who'd been holding the same pneumatic gun for too long, tightening the same eight nuts on a million half-built minivans as they floated by, one every 44 seconds, like a string of hollowed-out metal skeletons, maybe. If you've ever been in there you know what it looks like. Other guys got hurt in those nasty burn accidents down at the Ford Foundry where they used to stand on these little platforms while they poured the molten steel directly into the casings for the engine blocks. And there were some men and women who got permanently bent over from working at the trim plant, feeding those thick vinyl seat covers into a heavy-duty sewing machine.

For a while, a couple of years earlier, there'd been some fraud cases in the news and there was a lot of talk about how the whole Long Term Disability claims system was corrupt. GM hired a couple of private investigators to go around taking hidden pictures and videos of some of these broken-down guys who were supposed to be so permanently damaged they couldn't pick up a six-ounce wrench or sit in a chair pushing buttons for thirty-nine bucks an hour. They caught a lot of those guys on tape, banging out grand slam home runs and stealing a few bases in their beer-league softball games or going on ten-day fly-fishing trips with their buddies up in the Muskokas. They got one guy who was just bouncing on a trampoline in the backyard with his kids and another one who helped his neighbour build a deck, but that was enough to get them in deep trouble.

Musgrave lost a few customers after that crackdown, but most of the people I delivered to were the real thing, guys who just wanted to go back again and put on their safety glasses and their steel-toed boots and find another good spot on the concrete floor beneath the fluorescent lighting. For most of them, the ones who couldn't return, it wasn't about money. The LTD payments were big enough and they could go on forever, but without the job, the days spread out too far and there was nothing to look at. Lots of those guys pulled all the way back and faded out of the normal world. They changed their internal clocks and went on completely different shifts so they could stay up all night and not have to wake up again until one or two the next afternoon. Then they'd start it up right away with the gin and tonics as soon as they got out of bed, and by the time I came by with their packages some of them would already be half in the bag and they'd have to stagger out or kind of half-crawl to the door. The guys who lived alone were separated from their wives and could only see their kids every other weekend. They made their minimum support payments and dumped the rest into the cable bill and the big-screen TVs that took up half the wall in those little war-time houses on Rankin or Josephine. Some of those guys looked like they came straight out of the Hells Angels or the Desperados. They were way up over two hundred and fifty pounds and they had mean-looking goatees and shaved heads, but sometimes when I came by to drop off their medications, they'd be completely wrapped up in some mid-afternoon episode of *General Hospital* or pretending not to cry over the latest crisis on *One Life to Live.*

Most of my trips started with Barney. He was this horrible, fat, nearly naked guy and he had everything wrong with him. Diabetes, high blood pressure, kidney problems, a liver thing and some kind of circulation issue that made his feet swell up so badly that he couldn't wear shoes and could barely walk. Barney had been laid up like that for years and there was no chance he could ever go back to work. He even had one of those Medic Alert buttons that he was supposed to wear around his neck all the time and never take off. It had a flashing red light that told you the battery was okay and I guess if Barney ever felt himself slipping away, or if he felt his heart giving out or whatever it was, he was supposed to push that button and some kind of help would come screaming down the street to save him.

He was Musgrave's most regular customer and he was there with me from beginning to end, getting three or four deliveries every week. Barney had a standing account at the store and he paid for everything with a credit card over the phone so I never saw one cent from that guy, but that didn't stop him from piling on his extra stuff. He ordered from the pharmacy like it was a grocery store and every time I went to his house I'd have to haul a half-dozen heavy cans of Chef Boyardee. Musgrave kept it in stock just for Barney. Sometimes I'd catch him gobbling it down cold, straight out of the can.

In the summers, Barney used to sit outside on this one sagging lawn chair he kept on his front porch and in the winters you'd find him sprawled out on the couch in his front room

by the TV. Those were his only two places. He wore almost
no clothes, never any shoes, and usually just a pair of nylon
track shorts that almost disappeared when they got sucked
between the folds of his rolling gut and his wide, hairy thighs.
Once in a while he might pull on a short-sleeved Hawaiian
shirt that he would never button closed and when the real
humidity started up in July, Barney's whole body would get
this greasy sheen. A puddle of salt water would drip out of
him and pool under the lawn chair until it almost seemed like
he was one of those stinky, exotic plants from the rainforest
that need a heavy, regular watering every day.

He was famous mostly for his hernia. It was this red pul-
sating growth about the size of a misshapen grapefruit and it
bulged way out of the lower left hand side of his stomach. It
seemed like something impossible, like one of those gross,
special effects from an alien movie that was supposed to
make you think there was a smaller creature in there. Just
the shape of it, and the way it stuck out of him, and how it
seemed to come right at you, could make a person squirm if
they weren't used to it. But he refused to get it fixed and he
was always making a big deal about how tough he was and
how it didn't bother him at all. He thought it was funny to
pull back his shirt and scare the little kids as they walked by.

"It ain't hurting me," he used to say. And then he'd poke
at his own stomach just to prove it was true. The finger would
go deep down into the grapefruit and when he pulled it out,
the creature inside would kind of tremble.

"What do I care?" Barney used to say. "I'm not going to
lift another goddamn thing as long as I live and I'm not letting nobody cut me open."

The cops used to come around Barney's place every once
in a while to give him tickets for public drunkenness and disturbing the peace, but there was no way to really get rid of

him. All kinds of bad rumours circulated around his house and people used to say that Barney had a thing for kids and couldn't keep his hands off little boys.

During the last week of every month, or whenever the new issues came out, Barney would make sure Musgrave sent along the most recent copies of *Penthouse* or *Easy Rider* or *Swank*. He'd call it in early and by the time I finally made it to his house, he'd have been sitting there for hours, sweating it out in his slick, excited state, just waiting for me to show up. He'd pull the magazines out right away and start flipping through the pages and he always wanted to stretch out the spines and unroll the centerfolds to show me.

"Look at that one," he'd say and he'd hold up some crazed picture of an orgy that was supposed to be taking place in a working garage with five or six people, men and women, all tangled up around each other and bent over the hoods of the cars.

"You wouldn't have the first idea how to treat one of these ladies," he used to tell me. "You wouldn't have a goddamn clue what to do."

I made my own rules for Barney. He was always the first stop on my shift so I could get past him as quick as possible and outside of the most basic stuff, we never talked. When he tried to get at me with his pictures and his attitude, I never gave him anything to work with. To this day I bet he wouldn't know my name. I had to draw borders around him, safety zones, and when I brought over his stuff in the summer months, I only went as far as the top step of his porch and I stayed out in the open where everybody could see me. In the winter, I put down a hard line right at the threshold of his door. Even if it was driving snow or minus twenty or if the rain was coming down in heavy sheets – and even if he kept calling out from his couch, telling me to come in – I just stayed on my side and waited until he finally got angry enough to work up the guts and wince his way over to the door.

"You're a goddamned-lazy-ass-motherfucker, you know that?" he'd say as he grabbed the bag out of my hand and slammed the door in my face.

"You'd make a cripple walk before taking one step."

None of it fazed me. I might have my toes pressed up right against the sill, but I didn't cross over. I kept my distance and stayed out of reach and I never turned my back or gave him any kind of opening. It was the same thing every time. As soon as I made that turn onto his street, I started flipping through the different ways I could hurt him if I ever needed to get away. As far as I was concerned, it was self-defence and there was nothing Barney didn't already deserve, nothing that would be too much for him. If he made even one aggressive move in my direction, I'd unleash every jolt of energy I had. I could see myself screaming out for the neighbours and driving my foot straight into that hernia and scratching at his eyes. In my head, I had it set up like Barney's house was a kind of black hole that kept trying to pull me in and every time I left, it felt like I'd escaped again and I was free to go on for a whole other day.

*

The old ladies on my route were completely different and you couldn't say no to them. I might be the only person they'd talk to or meet face-to-face for an entire week and when I came to drop off their stuff they always wanted to have a real conversation and invite me in for a little visit.

"I have the tea all set up," they'd say as they came to the door.

In the winters, I'd have to take off my boots and leave them on a mat and then I'd go into the kitchen or the living room and sit down for maybe five or ten minutes, never more than that.

"You know I only have a second," I would tell them. "I have to keep going, you know. People are waiting."

"Yes, yes, of course," they'd say. "But God knows there's time for a little bite to eat, isn't there? And something wet just to keep you alive."

The snacks were all the same. There'd be a cool cup of tea with too much sugar in it and usually some kind of baked thing, a heavy piece of homemade pound cake, maybe, or a cold, rock-solid square with raisins in it that had just been pulled from a Tupperware container in the freezer. Probably a piece of cheese, too. I always tried to drink at least half the tea and eat half the square before getting up. I thought that was my part of the deal, like Santa Claus.

Their houses were full of family photographs. The late husbands and other relatives and shots of the grandchildren in their school pictures stared out at you from the shelves and the walls. They were all pretty much the same: the missing front teeth and the hair sticking up on one side, the bad teenage acne, the graduations and the weddings and the framed notices cut out of the paper for the twenty-fifth and the fiftieth wedding anniversaries and the obituaries. The kids were always sitting in front of the same pale background with the same pattern of pink and blue laser beams criss-crossing behind their heads. If you swung your head around the room, you could watch them growing up, getting fatter and more tired looking. Occasionally, the lady might give out a tidbit about one of them.

"Still in college," she'd say and she'd point at the serious-looking seven-year-old in his glasses. "When he was only

little, he used to say that we were 'best buds' and we had a little secret handshake we'd do whenever he came over."

"That one there is broken-up with her husband now and
the kids are ruined," she'd say, or, "Never been the same since
the accident," or "Now that she's got her fancy *la de da* house
in the country, we don't see much of her anymore."

I did a lot of favours for those ladies. Like if there was a
special Thanksgiving turkey platter up on the top shelf that
needed to be brought down or if there were hanging plants
that could use a little water, I'd do that. And I carried more
than my share of dripping garbage bags to the curb. They
were just little things, stuff anybody would do, but the ladies
always made a big deal out of nothing.

"Thank God you came by when you did," they would say.
"I'd never have been able to get that box of Christmas decorations out of the attic without you."

I tried to keep everything as light as possible and move as
fast as I could, but there were a couple of times when I was
stuck right in the middle of it – standing up on a chair in
the hall to screw in a new light bulb, or maybe stuffing a pile
of leaves into a garbage bag – and I would have to stop for a
second and slow everything down. It would just take a second, but I'd have to take a breath and maybe reach out a
hand to steady myself on the back of the chair or look away
from the leaves and up to the white sky to get my bearings. I
needed to get solid again and anchor myself against the bad,
dizzy feeling that used to wash up over me every once in a
while. It was one of those sick-to-your-stomach sensations,
the kind that hit you after a turn on the Tilt-a-Whirl, where
even though you're stopped and it's over and you're back on
the steady earth again, you still feel like your body is going
on without you and getting tossed around at some crazy
angle.

It seemed, sometimes, like I knew too much about things I wasn't really supposed to know at all. Like the first time your eyes touch on a bad case of bedsores – the kind that can eat big, fist-sized holes right through your flesh just from laying down in one spot for too long. The first time you see that, you can't look at anything the same way anymore. The Musgrave job was full of stuff like that. There was an old man who asked me to help rub in the eczema cream for his legs and when I kneeled down to touch him, even as softly as I could, large flakes of his skin came off in my hands like red fish scales. And there was another lady on McEwan who needed me to read her the fine-print directions on a package of glycerine suppositories.

"I don't know why in the hell they write everything so small," she complained to me while I waited outside the bath-room door. "Just tell me what it says. Are you supposed to run them under the water before they go in?"

I was like one of those guys in the audience who doesn't really want to be invited back stage, but then they shine the light on him and everybody claps and he has no choice but to get up and move behind the scenes, to the other side of that thick velvet curtain that normally hides all the secrets and keeps the magic going for everybody else. There was some knowledge you couldn't escape from. It came down on you like white water, flowing in only one direction, and once it got hold of you, there was no way to turn back and swim against the current. Even though I felt perfectly fine and my healthy twelve-year-old body kept pedalling hard between the stops, there were moments now when some image I didn't want would blow into my head and I'd think about the fact, the real fact, that there might be a day when I would not be able to stand up and close the drapes for myself. There might be a day when I wouldn't have the strength to walk across my own kitchen, and open the fridge and pick up the milk pitcher with one hand and fill up a glass I was holding in the other.

*.

The old ladies could teach you all about that stuff. They heard the way their kids whispered about what to do with mom, but the best of them stood up and just refused, just flat-out refused, to give up on their own places. From April to September, they'd be outside, digging through their gardens on their hands and knees and waving away the mosquitoes. And they still carved a pumpkin and had the candy ready for the trick-or-treaters, and lots of them even shovelled their own snow. It seemed like no blackness, no dirt or dust was ever allowed into their houses, that no rot or decay could even get a toehold.

Eighty-nine-year-old Mrs. Hume, my number-one favourite, used to come to the door, clear-eyed and busy and always a little annoyed by whatever it was that might pull her away from her work.

"What, what, what?" she'd say as she opened up.

I'd hold up the bag containing a refill of her blood thinners and she'd smile and say something like, "Oh, it's you again, is it? Well then, come in."

She'd be wearing one of her husband's old work shirts with a dish towel slung over her shoulder and some stiff wire brush in her hand and she was always in the middle of refinishing another piece of furniture. Her house was overstuffed with dressers and buffets and china cabinets that she'd rescued with her heat gun and her varsol and her twelve grades of sandpaper. I used to help her move them around, rearranging the rooms every couple of months, as though nothing could be allowed to settle into one spot for too long. We carried things evenly, with me taking only my half of the weight in the dresser. We'd both tuck our fingertips under the edge at the top and our shins would bang along at the bottom with every step we took, but we'd just inch our way along, taking little breaks whenever we needed to.

"Which one of these do you want?" she asked me once after we'd finally wiggled the sideboard into its new location. She waved her hand around in a semicircle and looked me straight in the eye without smiling. I could tell she wasn't joking, but at that stage in my life I don't think she knew there was nothing I needed less than a china cabinet.

"Which one?" she said again. "Just choose and I'll leave it to you in my will. I mean it. We'll write your name on a piece of paper right now and stick it in a drawer."

Once, when she was showing me one of her best little coffee tables, she explained it all to me.

"People are idiots, plain and simple," she said.

"I picked this guy right out of the garbage, for God's sake. I didn't even touch him after that. Just plunked him off the street and brought him right in. Just think about that for a second. They must be made of money. Idiots, I'm telling you. All of them."

*

But not everybody could keep it together like Mrs. Hume. I made lots of deliveries to elderly people who lived locked away from the world, up on the climate-controlled top floors of the assisted-living building for seniors on Riverside Drive. The staff tried to keep that place as cheery as they could. They had a bulletin board in the elevator that was full of photocopied notices telling everybody to come to Edith's big 95th birthday party – "No presents, just presence!" And there was stuff about the weekly card game every Wednesday in the common room and the movie nights and the special van that went on Sunday and made its own loop around to all the churches. You could get a regular ride to visit your friends in the hospital and, as long as the weather was okay, the van would go out to the cemetery every other week if you wanted it to.

But it always seemed like a dry place to me. Something about how they recycled the air made it feel like there was never enough oxygen in there. I couldn't breathe right and when I buzzed through the lobby and made my run through the building, I felt like I carried the weather with me, like I brought in the snow and the rain and the windy cold and they kept swirling around my body as I tracked wet footprints across the industrial carpets and down the corridors. Weather was the only subject all the residents cared about and I'd have the same conversation ten times in half-an-hour.

"And what's it doing out there today?" someone would ask as I handed over the calcium supplements. We'd be standing in the little living area that each of them had between the kitchenette and the bedroom, and maybe we'd both stare outside for a second, looking out through the thick glass of those unopenable windows. Down below, I could see where I'd locked my bike against a tree, but the street and everything that went on there seemed so far away that it was almost like we were stuck in a submarine or up in the space shuttle, and the world we were looking at had a whole different kind of atmosphere where we could never survive.

"Oh well," I'd say. Everything I ever said in the assisted living building started like that, as if the "oh well" was required.

"Oh well. The snow's starting now."

"It's cold then?" she might offer. "Getting very cold now? Making the turn into the real winter? You know, I haven't been out in a while."

"No," I'd say, trying to keep it as accurate as possible. Accuracy was what they wanted more than anything.

"No. Not too bad yet. Still have a few weeks before it really hits us. It's just a bit slippery now with the ice on the side of the road. Just slippery."

"Yes," she might say. "Slippery, yes."

Then there'd be a little cluck of recognition and you could almost see her thinking about it, about the word – slippery – and remembering the excitement and the danger that could be left over in a word like that, even in just the idea of it. Their apartments had all kinds of extra railings and there were suction cup bath mats and this special black tape they wound around door handles and banisters. Slippery wasn't allowed in the assisted living building.

The people in those apartments all had their little idiosyn-crasies. I remember the first time I realized it, the first time I really understood that, just like being young, there were lots of different ways a person could be old. Chatty or shy, out-going or held-back, risky or safe: everybody made their deci-sion and stuck with it right through to the end. There was a woman on the sixteenth floor who never unfastened the inside chain of her door. I probably delivered fifty packages to Mrs. Elson, but I never saw her entire face. When I came by, she'd give me only the smallest crack between the frame and her door and I'd have to squish the bag through to her. Then her thin hand would reach out with the money and I'd pass back the change. During the whole thing, I might catch only the quickest glimpse at the side of her head, just one un-pierced ear maybe, or that one eye staring out at me through the gap.

*

The half-blind woman on McKay could smell you coming. Or maybe it was the sound of the tire scraping the sidewalk. Before you could even set foot on the bottom stair of her porch, she'd start calling from deep inside the house.

"Door's open," she'd holler. "Just bring it right to me, dear. I'm in the back room. Last room at the back. Door's open. Just bring it to me."

Her voice was thin and kind of scratchy and it tugged me forward like one of those sticky threads that lead to the centre of a web. To get to her, I had to go down this long hallway, past the abandoned dining room on the left and the almost abandoned kitchen on the right. Her place was mostly dark and mostly empty and you couldn't block out the sound of her too-loud television and the smell of stale urine that had sunk down into the carpets and the cushions and mattresses. Her voice kept going all the time, like a homing beacon or a looping SOS that sends out the same message until somebody talks back.

"I'm right here, dear. All the way to the back. Just keep coming. Back, back, back. You can't miss me."

The sicker a person gets, the less of their house they use. It's usually the upstairs floors that go first, especially if the stairs are too steep and the railing isn't any good. Then it's the basement and then the back and front yards and then the whole outside just disappears. Some people used to ask me to look out the back window and tell them if the trees were still in the same places and if the tulips were coming up at the right time.

Eventually people like that spider lady on McKay got whittled down to one last room. It was usually a remodelled area near the back of the ground floor, a place big enough to double as both a bedroom and living room at the same time. There might be a new bathroom too, something roughed in by a caring grandson or a reliable nephew. I saw lots of places like that where a new toilet and a new vanity and a new low-rise shower sprung right out of the carpet like they'd been planted in the middle of the old den.

That woman on McKay ruled over her world in an automated La-Z-Boy throne. The chair could motor itself up and down and it was surrounded by four or five little tray tables that held everything she needed. There was a system to it, a spot for the remote controls and the telephone, and an area for lots of different boxes of Kleenex and a special corner for her purse and for those flip-top plastic tubes that keep all the pills for the week in separate little SUN, MON and TUE boxes. She had a place for her knitting stuff and one for the address books and the crossword puzzles and the Bible and another one for photographs. Even though she had cataracts and her sight was clouding over and her glasses were just for show, there was nothing she couldn't find. She kept her hair pulled back in a tight bun and though she never went outside, she wore real shoes instead of socks or slippers.

"I wonder could you do something for me?"

She asked me this once, during one of those 38 degree summer days where everything gets heavier than it should be. I was sweating from the bike and my shirt was damp and sticking to me. The smell in the room was thicker than normal. You could almost see it.

"Yeah," I said automatically. "No problem. What do you need?"

I pictured something like a bag of groceries that needed to be unloaded or a letter she wanted me to drop in the box.

"Will you look at this?" she said. "And tell me what you think I should do?"

159

Before I could get a hold on what was happening, she started to unbutton her blouse and to wriggle out of her sleeve and slide away the sturdy beige strap of her bra.

"Oh, no," I said, "Don't do that."

I turned in the opposite direction, toward the TV, but it didn't change anything.

"This isn't right at all," she repeated, "not at all."

It was like I was barely there and she was just looking herself over and privately keeping track of the changes in her body.

"You see how it's getting worse, don't you?" she said. "What do you think I should do? You work for the doctor's, don't you? What do you think?"

She'd pulled back her shirt far enough that I could see nearly her entire breast. It was a thin, used-up looking thing and almost the same white colour you'd link up with one of those ugly fish that live in some deep trench at the bottom of the ocean and have never seen light. The skin was criss-crossed with a purplish-blue network of veins and there were long, very long, black bristles growing around the nipple. Just below, you could see the problem – a big yellowish cyst, like the biggest pimple you can imagine, but circled in a dark red sore colour. It looked very bad, almost ready to burst and there was a shiny liquid film oozing out of it. The woman looped her index finger around the red circle and grazed over the surface in a tentative, worried kind of way.

"It hurts every time I move," she said. "Even when I'm just sitting in my chair. I thought it was nothing at first, but it's getting bigger every day and I can hardly stand it now."

It was the first time I'd ever seen one of those hidden parts of a woman's body – Barney's pictures didn't count for anything – and I didn't know what to do. I felt kind of dull and numb, like this was something I should have seen coming, but still couldn't prepare for. It was like when you get called up to the front of the class and they ask you to stare down the jumble of numbers and letters in a difficult math problem, but even before you stand up to go to the blackboard, you already know you can't do it, that this question is out there, beyond where you can go, and it's going to have to stay unsolved.

"I don't know," I said to her. "You need to see a real doctor. You need to get somebody to take you to the hospital and get looked at by somebody who knows what they're doing."

I told her I was sorry, and that all I could do was maybe check-in with the pharmacist when I got back to the store and that maybe if I described it to Musgrave and told him what it looked like, he might know what to do and maybe he would call her later on.

"Well that would be just great," she said, happier than she should have been.

"That would be wonderful, thanks so much."

"But it's the doctor you really need to see," I said. "You can't forget about that. You need somebody to take you to the doctor, right, as soon as you can?"

"Oh yes, yes, dear," she said. "I'm sure somebody will come along. No problem at all. Your Mr. Musgrave is going to call. He'll call and tell us what to do next."

Then she pulled her shirt closed and straightened herself up and slipped the buttons back together. It was all very matter of fact. A second later, she was thanking me again for all my help and telling me to grab a few cookies out of the cupboard on the way out.

"There might be a cold pop in the fridge," she said in a mischievous funny kind of way and that was that. One thing gave way to the next.

*

I worked my last day for Musgrave near the end of October, just after they turned the clocks back and everybody was still trying to adjust to the full dark coming down on them by five in the afternoon. The temperature dropped fifteen degrees in one night and there was a minefield of black ice on the side of the road. I zig-zagged across the city trying to avoid it and my eyes never moved from that spot a couple feet in front of the wheel. I'd been making my preparations for winter for the last few weeks and the fingertips were already cut out of my gloves and I was dressed in layers. All through September, it had been wet and rainy and my back tire had been kicking up a brown line of spray. Every coat I owned had this skunk-stripe of filth running down from my neck to the base of my spine.

When I made the turn to Barney's, the sky was still a little bit grey with leftover light. He was getting his standard package of canned goods and insulin and the little strips he used to test his sugar levels. There was a refill for his blood pressure medication and a roll of paper towels and a package of disposable razors. He'd already made his move off the porch and into the TV room where he normally sat with the remote in his hand and his legs spread wide over the velour cushions. I went up the stairs and knocked on the door and I called out to him, telling him that his stuff was here and that he better come and get it.

There was no sound from inside and I think that was the first sign I had that things were going to change. Barney was never not at home. I rang again and I rattled the front door a bit and I told him I'd just leave the package on the porch if he didn't want to pick it up. His inside door, the real wooden door, was wide open and there was nothing to keep me from just poking my head in and looking around, but I had those lines in my head and I stuck to the rules. I went over to the big front window and cupped my hands up against the side of my head and stared through the glass like a kid at an aquarium.

I saw Barney on the other side. He was still wearing his nylon shorts and his Hawaiian shirt, but he was down on the floor now, piled up in a fleshy lump and surrounded by newspapers and old magazines and take-out food wrappers. One of his arms was bent back at an angle that didn't seem right and his head was turned away from me so I couldn't tell if his eyes were open or closed. There was a bowl of Ravioli turned over near his head and the grainy red meat sauce was seeping into the carpet. It looked like all the hard stuff, all the bone and the muscle, had been sucked out of his body. The Medic Alert necklace was resting on the coffee table where he must have put it before he started eating and the steady red light kept blinking on and off like nothing was wrong.

My first thought was just to leave him there. I had my nose pushed up against the glass and I was only a foot away, but I couldn't shake this feeling in my stomach that this was how Barney did it. This was his master trick, his secret way of get-ting kids into his house.

"Barney," I yelled and I banged on the glass with my fist. "Get up. It's not going to work. I'm not coming in there."

But nothing came back from him. The shouting and the banging on the window didn't even send a ripple through him. I walked over to the door and I opened it again and stared in at him. The greasy smell of the house came out-side, but there was no sound and no movement. His body was just a thing, like a pile of laundry in the middle of the room, as still as the furniture. I think it was that stillness that got me. I was sure you couldn't fake it. A person just couldn't hold themselves forever like that. You couldn't do it on purpose.

I said his name again. I said "Barney" and I crossed over. It was like stepping out of an airplane.

Everything happened quickly after that. I walked over to the end table and pushed the red flashing Medic Alert button a couple times. Then it was only the two of us. I went over to Barney and rolled him over onto his back. His eyes were closed and everything had gone limp. Even the shape of his face was different and you wouldn't have recognized him. There was nothing left to hold him up from the inside and I didn't know what I should do. His body lumped in front of me like the low, half-built wall of a kid's snow fort, big enough so you could duck down and hide behind it. He was way larger than I realized and much softer and his skin was cooler than I thought it would be. There was a thin, white paste coming from his mouth and the head of his penis had flopped out of his twisted shorts. I put my ear down on his chest and felt his hair pushing against my cheek. I listened for a rattle or some kind of breath coming from way down inside of him and I ran my fingers around his neck trying to feel for the thudding or just a little surge of anything that might still be flowing through him.

I didn't have any training, but I set myself up for the kind of CPR I had seen on television. I tilted Barney's head back so his chin was pointed straight at the ceiling and I tried to flatten everything else out, his arms and his legs. I wanted to make sure all those hoses and pipes that I imagined running inside of him would be in line. Then I just did it and I put myself through a set of actions that would have been impossible to imagine five minutes earlier and were now just as impossible to avoid. I pinched Barney's nostrils together and brought my mouth down until my lips came right up against his. I held back for maybe half a second and then pushed down even harder until I had a tight seal over his mouth. It was simple after that. I blew my air into his lungs, sucking the oxygen out of myself and forcing it down into him. The taste of the ravioli and the beer and the white paste were still there in his mouth and I thought I might throw up when I lifted my head to pull in another clean breath. But then I went back down and I gave him two more breaths, as full as I could make them. Then I moved over to the middle of his chest and put my fingers together so my hands came down almost like one plunger pushing down on his round chest, squeezing at his heart ten or twelve or maybe fifteen times before I had to go back to the head and blow into him again. As I shuffled back and forth on my knees, moving just a couple inches from the top of Barney to the middle of him, it hit me that this was all it took. A person just needed the air to go in and go out and the essential liquids to go around and around. This was how they did it. This was how they kept your life going at the worst of times, by blowing it in and pushing it around and forcing it all the way through your body even if you didn't want or deserve it.

Everything worked exactly like it's supposed to. I kept it up with Barney for maybe five minutes, taking turns blowing and pushing, and then I heard the sirens. The ambulance stopped in front of the house and the flashing purple and red lights came in through the window. I looked over at the necklace again. It was still there, resting on the end table, still blinking on and off. I couldn't believe it had actually done what it was supposed to do. It was just a brown plastic circle in the middle of a beige plastic square with a piece of string attached to it and it didn't look like it had been cared for well enough to work. Then they were inside, an older guy and a younger woman wearing dark blue baseball caps, and they took over.

"Family?" the woman said to me as she unzipped her gym bag and started pulling out her gear.

"No," I said.

"How long have you been at it, approximately?"

"I don't know," I said. "Five minutes, no more than that."

She snapped on a pair of rubber gloves and took out a syringe and stuck it in a little vial and filled it halfway up with a clear liquid. Then, without any hesitation, without even changing the expression on her face, she found her spot and drove that needle right into Barney's arm and pushed down on the plunger with her thumb.

The man kept muttering to himself as he fiddled around with the wires and tried to untangle the paddles on his portable defibrillator.

"They never pack this right," he mumbled to his partner. There was a flat, bored sound in the way he talked and she just nodded her head and said the guys on the night shift were always like that.

It took him maybe fifteen seconds to get everything straight. And then it was just like you'd expect. The man pressed the paddles onto Barney's bare chest and the woman put her straight arm against my body to make sure I was standing far enough away. The man said "clear," very quietly as if there was really no one to warn, and then he sent a shock wave into Barney. It wasn't as loud as I expected. Just a sizzling sound and it made a kind of burning smell, but nothing happened. Then he said "clear" again and gave him another blast and that was the one that did it. Just like jumping a car after the lights have been left on all night. This big shiver went all the way through Barney's body and his face suddenly came back to its normal shape and he took in this enormous breath like he was coming back to the top of the lake after being under too long. He started coughing hard and spitting up. The woman rubbed her hand on his chest and she looked straight into his eyes. Then she looped an elastic band around the back of his head to hold the oxygen mask in place and she turned the dial. on a little tank to set the gas flowing. She shined a little pen flashlight into his eyes and started talking to him in this very slow, calm voice. She told him there'd been an accident, a cardiac event. But now everything was going to be okay. His signs were looking good, she said, and they were going to take him to the hospital.

"You are going to feel yourself being lifted," she said. "We're going to lift you and put you on a stretcher and take you in the ambulance. Do you understand what I'm telling you?" Her voice came out at that perfect pace.

"Just nod your head if you understand."

Barney nodded his head, but his eyes were panicked and they skittered around the room, clunking off the walls and the couch and the TV. Then he settled on me, the only person he recognized, standing about a foot away. All the confusion went out of his face and his expression changed back, back in one second, to the same angry and disgusted stare we saved only for each other. That's when he finally made his move on me. His arm shot up from the floor, faster than you'd think and he grabbed hold of my arm. He gripped it so tight, with so much pressure, it felt like he was going right through me and holding onto those two skinny little bones in the middle of my forearm. There was so much power in him, even then, so much strength in just one of his hands that I knew right away I would have never been able to fight him off. That was the only time we ever touched.

"It's okay," the woman told Barney in her soothing voice. "He's right here. Don't worry. He's not leaving."

Then she used both hands to pry open the trap and get my arm out. Barney kept staring at me all the time and I think he tried to say something, a word that fogged up the inside of his mask, but I couldn't make it out.

"Immediate family members can ride in the back of the ambulance if you want," the man said to me.

"He's not family," the woman said to her partner, and she pointed at me. "Just a bystander."

"There's no relation, right?" she asked again.

"No," I said.

"Well you can meet us at the hospital then," she said. "Hotel Dieu."

They covered him with a blue blanket and strapped him in tight and then they just rolled him out of the room and took him down the steps of his front porch. They loaded him into the back of the ambulance and the woman followed him in while the man went to the front to drive. I stood on the porch watching it all and she waved at me just before she pulled the door shut.

"See you down there," she said and they were gone. The rig pulled away without using the sirens or the lights and it slipped back into the new dark. They left me there standing in the middle of Barney's empty house.

There was nothing left to do. I went to the bathroom to splash some water on my face and rinse out my mouth and I was kind of surprised by how neat Barney kept everything in there. I didn't expect that he would have a bottle of liquid soap by the taps and a clean hand towel hanging on the rack. It was a kind of soap that we didn't sell and I pressed a couple squirts of it into my hands and rubbed them together under the warm water. Then I lowered my head a bit and I cupped my hands together and took a drink. The water swished around inside my head and I felt the faint taste of soap burning against my gums and the inside of my cheeks before I spat it out.

Then I went into reverse. I walked straight out and as I left the house, I turned the knob so the door would lock behind me. When I got back onto my own side, I looked down at the bag as it sat there, slumped on the porch and waiting for me. It was still full of all the orders for that day, all those little white packages, the things people needed. But it wasn't going to be my job anymore. I aimed the bike straight back to Musgrave and started thinking up how I would explain it all to him and break the news.

More than anything, I wanted to go home and be exactly my own age for as long as I could. That was my new plan. I would go home and lie on my bed and stare at the Guy Lafleur poster on my wall and love the way he didn't need a helmet. Then I'd eat nothing but junk – just Twizzlers and Blow Pops and Lik-M-Aid Fun Dip – and I'd listen to my music as loud as I wanted. Maybe I'd watch *The Dukes of Hazzard.* I thought about Bo and Luke Duke and how they never killed anyone and never used guns. Instead, they used to tape a stick of dynamite to one of their arrows and fire it straight into the bad guy's hideout and blast the whole thing into a pile of splinters and falling straw. That would be just about right, I thought. It would be great to just sit with them in the backseat of the *General Lee* and scream as loud as you could as they punched the gas and their orange car started up its long flight across the river, over to the other side, where no one could follow and you always got away.

Good Kids

If he is still alive – and there is no reason to think he wouldn't be – Reggie Laroque is probably close to thirty now. Maybe he still lives here, in the same city with the rest of us, or maybe it's Toronto now, or Calgary, or Cleveland. "We get around a lot," he told me once, when he was seven and I was twelve.

After Reggie moved out of the house across the road, the students came next and then the cats. A whole ragged, night-scrapping pack of them showed up one day and took over an abandoned car that had been sitting there for years, docked at the back of the driveway. The car was a four-door Chevrolet Caprice station wagon with all its tires missing. It had belonged to another former tenant, a long-haired guy who used to work on it in the evenings. One night, he moved away too and that was that. No one ever came back to claim the car for parts and nobody was going to pay to have it hauled off, so it just stayed there with its metal rims slowly grinding their way down into their masonry blocks. It seemed almost logical at first when the cats moved in, like the car was getting a second chance. Overnight it changed from a piece of junk into a sort of shelter. It stopped being a station wagon and became more like a cave, like something made of stone, a hole carved right into the earth that would never be moved. We called it, obviously, the "cat car" and after about a week, it became just another part of the landscape: a writhing, urine-soaked chunk of our terrain – almost entirely covered in hair.

171

The house across the way was the only rental property on our street. Its address was 237. My family lived on the even side, at 234, and if there was ever a mix-up, their mail might get accidentally delivered into our box. Mostly we got their bills with "Final Notice" printed in red ink and once in a while there might be a personal letter from someone whose messy handwriting made it difficult to tell the difference between the 4 and the 7. Whenever that happened my mother would make a special point of printing "wrong house" on the envelope before she gave it back to the mailman. She would use big block letters and press down hard with her pen, going over it two or three times, and underlining the word "wrong."

"That place is an insult," she used to say, peeking through the curtains.

"It's a revolving door. In and out, back and forth. No good for the area. Just you watch. When that place goes all to hell, it's going to drag us right down with it."

To us, 237 seemed like one of those doomed store locations that can't support any kind of business. All sorts of different people tried to make a go of it over there, but no one ever broke through. In the beginning there were a lot of quiet, single men, guys who never spoke to anybody and seemed utterly alone in the universe, but we also had a few couples and some families. They did what they could. In the springtime, somebody might get a surge of energy and they'd try and scrape off all the old paint and splash on a brand new colour, or maybe there'd be some flowers that would get planted in May, but never watered after that. A lot of things ended up half-done over there. The place was like a Bermuda triangle for hopeful people. No matter what they tried, it always seemed like the same persistent, revolving futility kept coming around to mow them down. Reggie was the only one who ever managed to hold if off.

He was younger than us, but seemed older. I'm pretty sure Reggie was one of those children who spent too many of his early years around adults and he ended up being more comfortable with grown-ups than he was with kids his own age. Everything about him was more formal than you'd expect. His hair was cut very short and he always wore a collared shirt that was tucked into his pants all the way around. He had a little brown belt and it went all the way around too, through all the little loops. He wore white socks and hard-bottom church shoes. When he walked up to us that first time, we were playing road hockey in the street between our houses and he just clicked-clicked-clicked his way right down the sidewalk, no problem at all.

"My name is Reggie," he announced, like this was a job interview. "Reggie Bartholomew Laroque."

Then he just stood there, perfectly still and patient, smiling and looking at each of us, waiting to see what we would do with this information. Long silences did not make Reggie uncomfortable. We kind of froze, trying to figure out the right response. He seemed like one of those religious people, like the child-version of one of those men in a white, short-sleeved shirt who can walk right up to your house, ring the doorbell and start talking to you about how to save your soul. My brother Matt slid over and put his hand up to my ear.

"Maybe he's retarded," he whispered. "Maybe he's slow."

I nodded my head a bit, but didn't say anything.

There are four boys in our family. I am the oldest and there's a set of twins in the middle – Matt and Christopher – and the youngest is James. During that time we spent with Reggie, we were all clustered in there between the ages of 8 and 12. This was right at the peak of our infatuation with hockey, when we cared about it in that total and absolute way that only kids can care about anything. None of us could skate, and we had never actually played in a real league on real ice, but we dumped everything we had into our games in the street. We built our own nets out of old two-by-fours nailed into posts and crossbars and instead of string netting, we used this heavy-duty industrial plastic sheeting that we had found behind a meat-packing plant. We cut the plastic and staple-gunned it right into the wood so that every time someone fired a ball into the net, it made a satisfying pop, like a burst balloon or a gun being fired. Our sticks were Koho and Sherwood shafts with plastic blades that had been wickedly curved over the front burner of the stove and we usually played with tennis balls that were too small and kept falling down through the grates of the sewer. We had the other kind of ball, too, a couple of those hard, orange, no-bouncers that are designed especially for the street and we believed that if one of those ever got fired straight into a guy's nuts, then that person would die. It became one of our most reliable standby threats – "I swear, I'll fire this fucking thing right into your fucking nuts if you don't fucking shut up." We had a pair of real goalie pads and a baseball glove trapper. For the blocker we used to spend five minutes taping an old phone book onto the outstretched arm of whoever was unlucky enough to play in the net.

"Can I join you," Reggie said. "Can I be a joiner?"

Right after his name, this was the first thing to come out of his mouth. I didn't think it was a big deal, and I was going to say no problem, but James was defiant from the start.

"It's two-on-two," he said, pointing at each of us and trying to make it clear. "Adding another guy will throw everything off."

James waved his hand at some of the other houses on our street where there were all kinds of kids who would have played.

"You find a friend and we'll go three on three," he said. "Three on three works."

Reggie never even considered it.

"No, no, no," he said. "That's fine. Forget it. Maybe I'll just watch. Is that okay with you if I just watch?"

He looked around and found a clean spot on the curb. Then he sat down and leaned forward with his elbows resting on his knees like this was Joe Louis Arena. When the ball went up on his lawn, he'd run and toss it back to us in the street and whenever somebody scored he'd say, "All right," but other than that he did nothing. You could tell that he'd never really played much of anything in his life. All his lines had been picked up from watching TV.

"Nice pass," he might say, or "Good execution."

The words he could use didn't match up with his body. It was like we had our own little Danny Gallivan there on the sidewalk, watching over us and rolling along all the time, keeping up a steady stream of compliments.

We showed off our drop passes for Reggie and our between-the-legs passes and the passes where we'd bank the tennis ball off a parked car. Sometimes we'd have break away contests or we'd use pop cans for targets and try to see who had the most accurate shot. Chris and Matt even used to practice their fighting. In the middle of a game they'd nudge each other and stare for that one dramatic second before they threw down their sticks.

"You wanna go? You wanna go me?" They'd scream at each other, trying not to laugh.

"I think those two are on the same team, aren't they?" Reggie asked, the first time he saw them shimmying around, trying to grab onto each other.

It didn't matter. One guy would try to trip the other or pull the shirt over his head and then, once he had the upper hand, he'd start pummelling away with these crazy exaggerated swings, piling on the furious, fake punches.

"Take that and that and that."

It was like those fights you see on pro-wrestling. The big, hollow blows kept coming down but there was never any real force behind them. Even if one of us caught the other in a crippling figure-four leg lock or if we slapped on the sleeper hold or a killer iron claw – a grip so dangerous it was guaranteed to cause permanent brain damage – it still meant nothing. All that rage washed over and left us completely untouched and unharmed and ready to go another round.

You hardly ever see big families like we had anymore. Especially not with boys. Today, if a couple has two or three boys in a row, they quit. I guess you could probably still make it through with four girls living in the same house, but I wouldn't know anything about that. Even back then we were different. From the outside we looked like good kids, like a bunch of those super-skinny, old-fashioned boys who might be headed down to the swimming hole in a Norman Rockwell painting. One of us was always in line to skip a grade – though none of us ever did – and we each had a paper route winding through the neighbourhood. One of us would probably mow your grass or shovel your sidewalk even though you didn't ask and if our school ever needed somebody to read something in public – at an assembly or a concert or a church service – we'd get that call. At Christmas, our parents made us collect cans for the needy and we grudgingly stuffed our quarters into the share-Lent pyramid that sat on our kitchen table during the weeks before Easter. When the nasty Greek couple who lived three doors down needed someone to look after their matching Pomeranians, Hector and Achilles, while they went back to Thessalonica for vacation, we said no problem. And when they came back and paid us only three dollars for the whole summer – three dollars for us to split four ways – we smiled and asked them to tell us all about the trip and to show us their pictures. It took a lot of consistent performing to pull this off, but it was like we couldn't help ourselves. We seemed exactly like good kids on the outside, but we weren't soft. There was more than enough hard waiting below the surface.

ONCE, WHEN I WAS ABOUT ELEVEN, I punched Chris in the face as hard as I could and there was no joke behind it. The whole side of his head swelled out with fluid and started to turn colour, a kind of reddish purple. We were home for lunch and it was some stupid confrontation about nothing in the backyard. I have no idea what it was about. He fell over and rolled around on the ground.

"I can't see. I can't see," he was crying. There was a little bit of blood in the corner of his eye.

My mother came out and shouted something about how this wasn't funny any more. She said that if we weren't careful somebody was really going to get hurt one of these times and then we'd be sorry. She put some ice on Chris's eye and she thought about keeping him home for the afternoon. But then the swelling was going down and she didn't want him to miss class, so she sent him back to school.

That was a mistake. Fifteen minutes after we returned to school, the principal called us both down to his office. We had never been in this situation before.

"How did this happen?" the principal asked me and he kind of waved at my brother's messed-up face. "Who hurt you, Christopher?"

"I did it," I said.

I did not cry, but it was almost there. It almost came through. All the possible consequences of the truth ran through my head. I thought about my permanent record and about what would happen if I was suspended or expelled.

"I hit him," I said. "It was an accident."

"See?" Chris said. "Like I told you, he's the one who did it."

"And you're both sure about this?" the principal asked again. The facts weren't working for him. He crouched down in front of me and pointed at Chris's face again.

"This doesn't seem like something you would do, Michael. Look at him. Are you sure there's no one else involved? You're not covering for somebody else? If something happened in the yard, you both need to tell me. Just give me the name. Tell me his name. You don't need to be afraid. You don't have to cover for a bully. I will not have violence in this school."

"No," I said again. "It was just me. Just us. I punched him at home in the backyard. I'm sorry it happened."

It took maybe one more second, but after that you could actually see the relief flowing into the principal's face. All the red drained out of his cheeks and he took a big breath.

"Okay then, okay," he said and he stood up and almost smiled. It was obvious that we had spared him from some complicated process involving letters and legal forms. I guess there must have been some kind of grade-school handbook that said violence was absolutely forbidden, but knocking out your sibling was still allowed. He looked at us and shook his head back and forth. I think he even laughed a bit.

"Lay off each other," he said. "Okay? I know how it is. I've got a brother. Everybody wants to kill their brother once in a while. Just take it easy."

Then he signed our little slips of paper and told us to go back to class and that was it. Not even a call home.

I'm pretty sure that Reggie was an only child, or that at least he didn't live with the rest of his family anymore. It was just him and his Mom in the house across the street and she must have worked afternoons or maybe midnights because we never saw her. We'd catch a glimpse of her coming and going maybe, but I never really met her until much later on. Reggie had his own key to let himself in and out and he took a lunch to school. He could do whatever he wanted.

Slowly, over a couple of weeks or months, Reggie wormed his way deeper and deeper into our lives. He'd sit on his porch in the morning and wait for us to come out and then we'd all leave for school together. And at recess, he'd find one of us and hang near by, never saying anything, just staying close. And he was always there for hockey after school. He spoke so well and he was so crazy polite all the time, that after a while, my mother was so impressed she invited him over for dinner. She asked what his favourite food was and he said cabbage rolls. He could have had anything and Reggie chose cabbage rolls. It wasn't something we normally ate, but my mother found a recipe and did her best with it. After about a month, our schedule was set: every Tuesday night we had him over for cabbage rolls.

"If your mother says it's okay, Reggie, you can come over and have dinner with us tonight if you'd like," my mother would say. And then she'd wait for it.

"Well, that depends," Reggie would say, grinning because he fell so easily into this kind of back and forth with adults.

"What will you be making tonight?"

"I was thinking about cabbage rolls. How does that sound?"

"Wonderful," he said. "That's great. Cabbage rolls are my favourite meal."

It was the cabbage rolls that turned everything around. I hated them: the sour smell, the squished rice, the slimy green shell. Once, during one of those dinners, I leaned over to Matt and whispered, "I can't eat this shit anymore."

I pointed my fork at Reggie on the other side of the table, but I didn't think it was obvious.

"He's starving me right out of my own house."

Matthew smirked a bit. But when we looked up, it was over. My mother had her teeth gritted together hard and she was shaking her head back and forth.

"Go," she said. Kind of quietly at first, then louder.

"Get out of here, right now. The two of you. Get out of my sight."

She threw her fork down onto the plate and stood up, pointing us out of the kitchen.

We had to wiggle past Reggie's chair to get out from the table and then we were face to face to face with her.

"Sometimes I wonder where you come from," my mother said, talking directly to me. "Sometimes I think I've wasted all my time on you."

She was so angry or so disgusted I thought she was going to lose it right there in the kitchen in front of him. I thought maybe she was going to cry or hit us like she sometimes did when she was so frustrated she didn't know what else to do. My father, who'd been quiet throughout the whole thing stood up beside her and as we went by, he sort of shoved us along the way upstairs. When he looked at me, it felt like his eyes were pushing mine into the back of my skull.

"Yeah, you're starving, aren't you," he whispered and he rubbed his forehead with his fingertips and then kind of pinched the bridge of his nose. He was trying hard to keep it under control. "You're starving. Right."

After that it was obvious that nobody could touch Reggie while he was in our house. My parents made sure we left him alone. Outside though, things were getting worse. At school, Reggie didn't have anybody so he used to cling to us as if we were his best friends. It was okay for me because I was so much older, and I could just ignore it, but it was killing James. Other kids started to tease him about Reggie, asking if Reggie was James's new girlfriend and singing stupid rhymes about Reggie and James sitting in a tree. It got to be too much – it seemed that nothing worse could happen to a kid that age – and one day James turned on him.

"Listen," he said as we were all walking to school. "I don't want you hanging around with me anymore. You have to get some other friends."

"I don't want to," said Reggie. "I don't like them. I like you guys and I like your mom and I like your dad. And that is everybody who I like. That's it. Nobody else."

"You don't get it," James said slowly. "Leave me alone. Do you understand? Stay away from me."

"I'm not going to leave you alone. Even though you say so, I don't have to," Reggie said. "You can't make me. I'm going to stay, and if you try to make me leave then I'll tell on you. I'll tell your mother and your father."

We were all caught off guard, but since James was the one talking, he just went nuts.

"You will so leave me alone, you little shit, you little fucking retard," he said.

"Leave me alone. Leave all of us alone. Don't you get it? None of us like you. Don't you get that yet? Leave us alone."

"No," said Reggie. "No."

It was just short and simple like that and you could tell he wasn't even angry. It all just bounced right off him. Like he heard it, thought about it, and decided not to take it. He turned and sort of skipped off along the way to school and after a couple steps he turned back and looked right at James. He kind of sang at him in a teasing voice, "No-no-no, No-no-no."

That cracked it wide open. James took off after Reggie and he tackled him in the front yard of this house and he started hitting him hard in the stomach and in the face. They were rolling around and then James was on top, kneeling over him, pinning Reggie's arms with his knees and he was belting him with his closed fists. Then he got up and started kicking Reggie in the arms and then up around his neck and his ears and then right square between the legs as hard as he could.

"Fuck you, fuck you, fuck you. Leave me alone," James said. And even though Reggie was getting pounded, he still kept talking back, stuttering through it.

"It doesn't hurt, doesn't hurt." he said. "No . . . no . . . no. Doesn't hurt."

Some people think that when kids fight it's just cute or funny, but that's only because they've never really seen it. They've never seen how, if the timing is right, it's like an electric current is being fired right through the body of a little boy, like he's been electrocuted and this jolt is ripping through every bit of him. James was like that with Reggie and it was not cute or funny. I think it was the only time, the only time that any of us, any of my brothers, ever got in one of those bloody, drag down, if-I-had-a-knife-I'd-stab-you-in-the-eye kind of fights with someone who wasn't one of us. We did it to each other every once in awhile, but this was the only time we went after somebody separate, somebody we didn't have to come back to in the end.

By the time Matthew and Chris and I ripped them off each other they were both a mess. It had poured rain the night before and it was still early in the morning so the ground was all sloppy and greasy. James was covered. His pants were wrecked, all green and brown around the knees from when he had been kneeling over him and his shirt was stretched out of shape, and ripped a little bit around the neck. There was this thick wet mud all over his face and his hands.

Reggie was worse. Because he was lying on his back, all the blood from his nose was smeared out across his face. It ran back towards his ears and up into his hair and down into his mouth in these long, long spidery thin lines. It was like his face was a window and someone had thrown a rock right through the middle of it. When Matthew first looked at him, he said, "Holy Fuck, we have to take him to the hospital right away."

Then he turned on James.

"'Look what you did to this little kid,'" he said. "We have to go to the hospital now. We're going to get killed for this. All of us, you know, not just you. We're all dead for this one."

He was wrong. In the end, it turned out that we weren't all dead because of this. We weren't ever even going to hear about it again. We didn't have to call an ambulance and we didn't have to go to the hospital and we didn't have to fill out a report because, in the end, it turned out that Reggie was fine or he at least seemed fine or he pretended to be fine. When we got James off him, he jumped right up and he said, again, "No, no, no. We're all right, don't worry."

He didn't cry once and even though, as I was watching it happen, it looked like he was really getting the snot beat out of him, now, I thought that maybe Reggie had been telling the truth all along and that it really didn't hurt, didn't hurt.

It was like all that pounding hadn't got anywhere near the centre of him.

He got up, walked out into the street and crouched down near a big murky brown puddle that had formed the night before when one of the sewer grates backed up. Then he cupped his two hands and he dipped them deep into that solid brown, grit-filled water as if it was a completely normal thing to do, as if this was a pure white sink in a pure white bathroom. He pushed his face into it, rubbed his palms up and down and then used his fingertips to work the dirt out from around his eyes and the blood from under his nostrils and down by his mouth. He splashed some into his hair and tried to smooth it down back to normal.

James was the one who turned scared now. He sat there, on the soaking wet ground, dazed and crying these soft little really sad cries, almost whimpering. Reggie called him to come over to the puddle and James got up and went straight over.

"I'm sorry, Reggie, I'm so sorry," he said, all runny-nosed and crying and dirty. "Please don't tell anyone, okay. I'm so sorry, please don't tell anybody."

"Don't worry about it," Reggie said. He was flat and calm now. Every second he was coming back closer and closer to his normal self. His face was almost okay, a little puffy maybe but getting there.

"I won't tell anybody," he said. "It's okay. I know you didn't mean it. But we have to get cleaned up right now. You and I have to get cleaned up or everyone will ask what happened."

A second later James was doing the same thing. He was in there, in the puddle, scrubbing his face and his arms, trying to get the dirt out from under his fingernails.

Reggie said, "Face and hands. You just got to get your face and hands looking all right. For the rest you can just say you wiped out somewhere. No big deal. Come on now. Let's see what you look like now. Let me get a good look at you."

James stopped washing and he turned toward Reggie. And Reggie put his two hands on either side of James' face. And then he untucked his own collared shirt and started to dry off James' face with it, wiping around in soft circles.

"There you go," he said, "All better. Good as new. You look fine to me."

The two of them walked over to a car and looked at their reflections in one of the side mirrors. Then he turned to us.

"You guys go on," he said. "Then we'll come in a second. No need to make a big show."

That's what I remember most clearly about it, that last part, with Reggie bossing us around, solving it and telling us what to do next. The rest of us, even me, way older than he was, we did exactly what he said and went to school. I turned my back and I left him there with my little brother. I let him work it out all on his own.

AFTER THAT, things were different between us, between the four of us and Reggie. He played road hockey with us all the time now with our uneven teams, our three on twos, and it really didn't matter. We lent him a pair of old sneakers and it turned out that he wasn't that bad at all once he got the hang of it. He still went on with the cabbage rolls and the rest of it, but everything was different.

Through the remainder of the fall and into the winter and on past Christmas it went pretty much the same. Then in January and February it started to get too cold outside so we had to move everything in. Down in the basement of our house we started this intricately-organized league of tabletop gear hockey. We kept stats and we followed a schedule, and

we posted our rankings on a piece of Bristol board taped to
the wall. For about a month that was all there was, thinking
up clever passing plays, sawing back and forth with those
metal rods and working on our one-timers from the back
defenseman. Reggie was great at this kind of hockey. When it
came to pushing those little plastic guys around, and shoving
the goalie back and forth in his limited little one-line crease,
nobody was better. We also watched a lot of games on TV. It
was that period of New York Islander and Edmonton Oiler
dominance, a terrible time to live where we lived. It might
have been great on the Prairies, but around here the Red
Wings and Maple Leafs were both terrible. It was the John
Ogrodnick, Rick Vaive era, a time when halfway decent guys
like that could score fifty goals on a team that didn't have a
chance of making the playoffs. They were so terrible we
didn't expect anything from them and we could just sit there
and watch our nothing teams doing nothing in a game that
meant nothing. Reggie was absorbed right into that. He still
never slept over and he only ate with us on Tuesdays, but
when I think about that time, I remember him always being
there, sitting on the couch with us or getting ready to drop
the puck out of his left hand while the fingers of his right
swivelled the centre man and set him up for the face off. The
coldest weeks passed quickly and it wasn't long before we
were back outside in the spring and starting to think about
baseball.

Then one day after school, in April or May, I think, I
answered the door. I opened up our front door and that
ended it. I barely recognized her because I had never really
seen her close up before. She was wearing white sweatpants
and white running shoes and one of those blue nylon wind-
breakers that folds neatly into a pouch. She seemed very
skinny to me and her hair, which was pulled back into a

ponytail with one of those pink bobble elastics, was that colour that goes right in between blonde and brown. I remember that she was wearing a lot of makeup so her face looked more dressed-up than the rest of her, and I couldn't decide if she was a young person who looked old or an old person who looked young.

"Is Reggie home?" she said, sort of tentatively and just from the way she said his name, just from the way she said "Reggie" I knew that he belonged to her.

I stood there with the doorknob in my hand, and, for a second, I tried to figure it out. I tried to run through all the possible explanations for her and for Reggie. I tried to imagine what they ate on all those other nights, and what shows they watched together, and why they had moved here in the first place and why, after all this time, she was finally here, standing on our porch. I looked at the Velcro straps on her white sneakers and I wondered if it meant anything if a grown-up lady wore Velcro shoes and jogging pants while her son only wore dress clothes. For a little while, I thought maybe this was a clue for something else, the key detail in a sinister mystery I was supposed to solve, but after two seconds, I decided it probably wasn't. I didn't know what to do.

"Dad," I said. "There's somebody at the door for you."

"No," she looked at me and whispered it kind of frustrated. "I want Reggie."

But then my father was there and my mom came right behind him and the two of them stood there with me on our side of the threshold.

"Is Reggie home?" she asked again. And my father answered right away, "Yes, yes he is, just a second."

He went over to the basement door and called for him to come up.

"Just one second," Reggie's voice came back. You could tell he was concentrating on something else and didn't want to be distracted.

"Just one more second," he said.

"No, Reggie, come right now," my father said. "Stop playing and come right now."

Then he turned and shook hands with Reggie's mom. He told her his name and said it was nice to meet her. And then my mom did the same thing.

"Your son is a very nice little boy," she said. "You've sure done a good job with him."

"Yes," my dad agreed. "That is a very nice little boy you have there. A very kind, very generous boy. He has never been a bit of a problem to us, never made even a little bit of a fuss."

He spoke slowly, like he was trying to make sure it got through, and she looked at him very carefully and nodded her head slowly.

"Yes," she said, "I know. Thanks. Thanks for you guys too. He likes you, you know. You're all he ever talks about over there. Thanks for being nice to him and thanks to your boys, for playing with him, and being nice to him and taking care of him and everything."

And then Reggie was there and the rest of them had come up the stairs too. I don't know what I expected or what I wanted, some big moment maybe, but nothing happened. When Reggie saw his mom on our porch, he ran right over to her with this big smile and gave her a hug. Then, he showed us off, one at a time, and did the introductions all over again.

"Yes Reggie," she said patiently. "I know. I already talked to them. Come on, we have to go home now."

"Okay," he said and he ran and got his coat and then he was gone.

"See you later," he said and the two of them went back across the street.

They left in the middle of the night and I think there must have been a problem with the rent because the house was empty for the whole summer and the landlord never took in another family after that. He got greedy and that's when he started rotating the students through, a different bunch every year. They came and went so fast you could never keep track of who was really living there and he packed them in so tight, there must have been eight or ten guys crunched in there at the same time. For the first few weeks, we could still pretend the students were just a set of temporary stand-ins who were only going to hang around for a little while until the real permanent replacements arrived, but then they let one of the front steps rot right through and the grass went a whole year without getting cut. Even before the cats arrived, I could tell that things had changed for good and that Reggie probably wasn't going to come back and fill us in with all the details about this great trip he went on with his mother and all the adventures they had along the way.

The students were all the same, very nice and polite if you met them in the daylight hours when they were on the way to class, but not so good at night. Everything about them was so obvious. They piled up a monument of their accomplished empty beer cases on the front porch and they had curtains made of Confederate flags and Union Jacks hanging in their windows. If they had a particularly good night, a flock of stolen pink flamingos might end up perched on their lawn in the morning. I remember a time when they hauled off one of those heavy-duty steel newspaper boxes from a street corner, the kind where you're supposed to put in your money and they trust you to take only one paper. The box must have weighed a couple hundred pounds and we had no idea how they had managed to carry it all the way home. For a while they worked on it, trying to crack open the lock with a screw driver or saw through the steel casing so they could get into the part where they'd get rich on a couple rolls of quarters. Eventually they gave up, but the box stayed there on the porch right beside the beer cases. In big letters it said, "Get the News Here."

They did the normal things: taped a long, larger-than-life poster of a swimsuit model on their front door, played their music too loud, watched horror movies or porno flicks late at night with all the windows open. Those guys would pee on your lawn at one in the morning and then throw-up on your lawn at four. And they'd never apologize. They seemed to get off on the whole public display of it.

"Someone should call their parents," my mother said once, sneering again as she stared across the street. "I don't care how old they are and I don't care if they do go to the college. If those were my boys behaving like that – if that was you over there – I'd give you such a thrashing you'd never forget it."

When we were finally forced out, it took us almost a year and a half to get rid of the house. My parents hired a real estate agent, a lady with tight curly hair who wore a lot of heavy jewellery and seemed to own a never-ending series of matching pant suits. She had a sign with a glossy picture of her face on both sides and she hammered that right into the middle of our front yard. After the first few months passed without any offers, she told my parents the house wasn't selling because we lived in what she called a "mixed neighbourhood" and that nowadays most young families wanted to raise their kids in a quieter type of place, somewhere with a nice backyard and maybe a deck.

"Look around," she said and she stood on our porch and

waved her hand in a slow semicircle from one end of the street, past Reggie's house, all the way to the other side, like she was giving a tour and wanted my parents to drink in the beautiful scenery. Everything was quiet.

"We have to be realistic," I heard her say, in one of those too-loud theatre whispers. "You know how it is. There's only three things that really matter: location, location, and location."

She suggested a new asking price, a much lower number for my parents to think about, and she told them time was already tight.

"We have to get while the getting's good," she said. "Or you could be stuck here forever."

My parents stared at her and didn't say anything. Then my dad reached out and he squeezed my mother's hand and they sat down on the step close to each other and stayed there for a while, thinking it all the way through. The real-estate lady said she wouldn't leave without a decision and she stood over them, reciting a list of all the things that were wrong but could not be changed. Our bedrooms were too small and the basement was too low and there weren't enough cupboards in the kitchen. The furnace was on its last legs and the shingles were pretty well shot and no one, no one anymore, could live in a house with only one bathroom. She was one of those sales people that everybody hates, the kind who can guess how much you make in a year just by looking at your shoes. She'd been through this before, hundreds of times, and she understood the choices. Now it was only waiting. I watched her sliding her eyes up and down over my parents and my brothers and our house and all we owned and I could tell that she thought she had us figured out completely.

The Number Three

The single fried egg might be life's loneliest meal. He listens to the sizzle of unfertilized yolk and waits another second before lifting away from the heat. The timing is important. He wants the skin starting to harden but everything else still shaky and runny inside. It quivers on his spatula before sliding onto the plate slimy and wet, like a living thing. Half a shake of salt, a full shake of pepper and good to go. This is supper. The toaster pops and he looks over. Watches the filament cooling, turning black again. He butters and dips and mops. The room is almost silent. Only the occasional gurgling coming from deep inside the fridge. A single fried egg, he thinks: enough food for one person, as long as they aren't hungry.

He checks the cordless telephone again but there is no change. The phone is a smug little bird that refuses to sing. Words on its tiny screen say *No new messages*. There is a button for *Talk* and a button for *End*. *Redial* and *Flash* and *Clear* and *Mute*. Nothing from it all day. He looks at the calendar. One day until the day. Already one year. It goes and comes so fast. Only these hours left. You better call. He says it out loud. You better know what you need to do.

The house is too big for him now. He feels like the marble in one of those tilting wooden labyrinths and he has to try not to bang off the walls or fall through the holes. The space is crowded with things that should have disappeared, a thousand items that should have been wiped away and deleted, all at the exact same moment, while the body was flying through the air. Instead, they stayed and registered nothing.

When it gets like this, the kitchen is worse than the bedroom. More intimate. Always something else waiting behind a cupboard or rolling loose in a drawer. *The World's Greatest Mom* mug – a last-minute gift from a lazy kid – hanging on its hook. And stuck behind a magnet is the reminder card for a dentist's appointment they never made it to. The secretary from that office left messages for a month, trying to reschedule a semi-annual cleaning. The boy's favourite deep cereal bowl and her preferred paring knife, the only one that stays sharp.

Scattered clothes and mismatched socks. Filthy T-shirts he washed only eight months later when the last of the smell was gone. The bristles of their toothbrushes, fanned by his thumb. Her half-completed plan for renovating the basement. Magazines flopping through the slot every two weeks. *Style at Home* and *Canadian Living*. His son's password-protected laptop. He knows there are messages in there.

His daughter, the one who wasn't there, the one still left, says he needs to get out. Find something smaller, something more manageable. Maybe a condo downtown. A place where no one has lived before. Walking distance to everything from there. Think how much better that would be.

When it was all over and they finally let him out of the hospital, she took a semester off from her school in Kitchener. They tried to fill in the blanks and get their rhythm back, tried to live as close to the original pattern as possible, but even while it was happening, he knew it couldn't last. A girl, a woman in her early twenties, must go back to what she is. Things have to be done when they need to be done and the somewhere-else schedule will not wait. Friends and paper deadlines, she says. Assignments and exams. Picking up extra shifts at the restaurant. Been very, very busy these last few days.

She calls twice a week now. Usually Wednesday nights and Sunday afternoons. Usually on her cellphone. How are you, Dad? He hears other voices in the background. Are you in a car? he asks. Are you driving? Don't talk to me while you're driving. I'm hanging up right now. Pull over and stop and talk to me then. Not driving she says. God. Just a bad signal. Sitting in a restaurant. Poor reception. Then five dutiful minutes of their voices passing each other on a satellite network. I have to go, she says. Love you.

He picks up the receiver and hits *Talk*. They say it works both ways, but this is different. He would go with her if she came to pick him up. He would make an exception for her. Tomorrow will always be a different day. The dial tone comes through steady and clear and he puts the sound up on the speaker. If you listen carefully you hear a clacking in the background, behind the tone, something like a train. He puts his ear toward it, straining. Feels like he is getting close to something before a quick ring cuts in. A ring inside the dial tone. A message from the phone itself. A stranger's voice, a man who seems official. He says: If you would like to make a call, please dial a number. If you need help, please hang up and dial your operator. The voice starts to say it again, but the phone cuts him off. The phone cuts itself off. The phone is frustrated with this situation and cannot allow it to continue. A high pitched squealing rises. Like talking to a fax machine. Then a hard, extra loud busy signal. Bomp bomp bomp bomp. He hangs up. Pushes *Off.*

Anniversary, he thinks. It makes him so angry. Parents and their kids, nothing can be done. Connected and separated, different ages at different times. They can never really live together. By the time they are who they are going to be, they're gone. He thinks about the fundamental difference between remembering and being reminded. The next time they talk, she will say something about how she lost track of time, how she was in the middle of it, squeezed up against an immediate pressure that blotted out everything else and she simply forgot. She will likely cry and she will be so, so sorry, but it already makes him feel sick. Jesus Christ. A person should know where they need to be and when they need to be there.

He listens to the forecast, takes out his map of the county and studies the Number Three. An inch here is equal to two miles there. He measures with a ruler, estimates distance, and considers the problem of travel. How to pull it off. Probably close to thirty miles, definitely more than twenty-five. It will take some doing, but if she doesn't call by tonight, then that is it. He will go by himself.

*

It felt like rescue in the beginning. Ninety days in and a chance at safety for the rest of their lives. A guaranteed spot on the seniority list as long as he kept up his end of the deal. Collective bargaining, the way work works. It meant everything for them. Getting in and hooking up for the steady ride and a reliable flow. Pure blind luck. He was hired off the street, plucked away from the rest of the world and delivered from what other people have to do to make a living.

We can go for another now, can't we? She whispered it in his ear. It was the night of the ninetieth day. Their girl just three years old, still sleeping in a toddler bed. Yes, he said. Her hand moving under the sheets. Tingling in her voice. His eyes on the ceiling before he rolled his knee against her thigh.

Yes, he said. It was the night of the ninetieth day. I think we're going to be okay.

Around here, nineteen-eighty-three is the year that counts and that is where the line should go if they ever write a history of this place. This was long before he started, years before they got in, but nineteen-eighty-three matters for everybody. The way it came along and shook up the whole domestic side of the business. Lee Iaccoca taking a risk. The famous picture. His not-so-confident smile as he stands there at the Auto Show in front of the first generation. The paint they used to have. That in-between shade of maroon and a strip of Wood-grain paneling running down the side. It was the last of the real game-changers and they decided to build it here. Some-body's arm got twisted on that, a face was pushed up against a wall. He knows that, thinks about it sometimes, the question of origins. Why it is where it is. The first one, the one in the picture, it's in the Smithsonian now.

It goes by different names. The *Magic Wagon* or the *Grand Caravan*. The *Voyager* or the *Town and Country*. Chrysler, Dodge and Plymouth. The customer picks the model and the trim package. A hood ornament that holds the eye. Chrysler looks like a star that lives inside your house. His daughter used to say that. His son drew pictures of the long-horned sheep. A Dodge is *Ram Tough* and always red. Plymouth is more mysterious: a silver ship with wind in its sails. What is that supposed to be exactly? The Mayflower, he thinks. The Mayflower landing on Plymouth Rock. A car for pilgrims. Word associations that don't quite hook up. None of it mat-ters. The company will sell it any way you like, but it is always the same underneath. You do not fool around with a machine that works.

He has seen enough of them to know that there is no secret behind the Grand Caravan. It is exactly what it appears to be, an object designed to fulfill a basic need for a reasonable price. In the beginning, the sliding door was its signature. The way the whole side of the car could detach and roll along its track to give you such a large opening, even with only six inches of clearance on the side. A big door that wouldn't bang against all the other doors in the mall parking lot and enough room inside for seven people and all their stuff. Those were the original brute facts, the Caravan's simplest truths. Parents and kids piling in and out all the time – the soccer mom, yes, the soccer mom – but a seat for the visitor, too. A place for grandma when she has to be picked up at the airport. The driver and passenger up front and two benches in the back. You click down and the rows pop out. No points for style, but versatility has always mattered for this segment of the market. You take out the seats and there's enough space back there for a 4x8 sheet of plywood. A plan for all the standard dimensions. He knows nothing fits together like that by accident.

People in the city feel the car in different ways. The Caravan goes past the men and women who work in the plant, beyond Chrysler and the CAW and Local 444. It moves over his family to reach everybody else. The guy who sells carpeting or the orthopaedic surgeon or the lady who teaches grade two French immersion. They all know. They can tell when things are going well and when they aren't. They understand the way it sits on every bottom line.

It was the number-one selling minivan all by itself for more than a decade. The number-one selling vehicle for the whole country. Took years before the Asians caught up. Millions rolling away from this spot. They build it on the S-platform, then the AS, then the NS, then the RS and the RT. It started with a piece of crap 2.2 litre in-line 4 with barely 85 hp and that weakling would whine and complain and shake like you were re-entering the earth's atmosphere every time you pulled into the passing lane. Now you go for the optional 4-litre turbo-charged V6 with 251 hp and that monster can pull your whole crew and all their bikes and your little hardtop camper up a mountain in the middle of July. He liked to watch the temperature gauge whenever he took theirs out on a long trip. The way it never budged and always stayed straight up, right in the middle, balanced between the red hot H and the cool blue C. He used to think that was all a person could ask from a car. An engine that was ready when you called.

The way it comes together is something to see and he has never taken it for granted. The interconnecting lines of yellow and orange conveyors, bodies and chasses moving separately before they mate. The bright white lights in paint, the orange robots swivelling in for their welds. The flash and the flash again. He used to think you could count the individual sparks and always arrive at the same number.

People outside think people inside must hate the machines, but it's not like that. The Local has to fight for every job, but precision is precision and a person working on something likes to see it done right. When he watched those hydraulic shoulders rotating, lifting 1,300 pounds and holding it perfectly still, always within the same range of a hundredth of a millimetre, he felt something, but it wasn't hatred; it was more like confusion or a stab of deep-down uncertainty. It gets confusing after awhile if you have to watch a robot work and you watch it and you watch it again. The repeating sequences start to blur and it seems like time stops and there is only this one task left in the whole world, this one job, separated from everything else, and it has to be done again and again, forever. The robot sees a hundred divisions in a millimetre and it always hits the same spot. The same weld. The same number of sparks.

A standard dash assembly comes as a single unit. It moves on a hydraulic but has to be guided into its spot by hand. You need to feel it in. An engineer told him once that they were decades away from creating a robot that could mimic the instinctive muscular adjustments of the human wrist. The engineer swivelled his hand around a couple of times. Think about this thing, he said. The wrist. You can't imagine the number of interrelated calculations. The way it pulls together force and angle and time, the way it cross-references. Makes it look easy, but never the same way twice. Can't replicate intuition. A bolt. An infinity of bolts tightened just enough. Not too far and not not far enough. A car is held together, fastened more than assembled.

They think of everything. The big stuff and small stuff, it all matters. Subtle cosmetic redesigns for the interior and complete retoolings. Power windows and locks. ABS. The new transmission. The second sliding door. Keyless entry and remote starter. The new suspension. Standard air bags – multistage and curtain – even in the base model. Five-star safety. Side impact beams. Always tweaking the engines to find a little extra. Before the gas got crazy, 20 miles a gallon in the city wasn't so bad. Stow n' Go seats rolling straight into the floor. Swivel n' Go seats spinning around. A built-in card table. Two different DVD players for the kids showing two different movies. Everybody gets their own headphones. Nine cupholders. Chrome accents. They move the shifter off the column. They fix the clock. Put in the MP3. The GPS. Every small change in the finished product is a bigger change on his end.

He liked to ride along sometimes as the next one rolled off the line and into the world. He liked to be the first person to read the cooing odometers with all their 0's in a line. A fully loaded special edition Town and Country with the windows that go down in the back to let the fresh air get in. One minute in there and you know. They flick the wipers, honk the horn two times and flash the brights just before it leaves. When it passes the last inspection, it gets the all clear and begins its life. He liked moving inside his work and feeling it moving around him. He liked understanding the interconnected parts and being the first to look through a clean windshield and see everything from this point of view. You cannot beat a brand new minivan. Ask around. Ask anybody. A person appreciates being up high when they're driving.

There are gaps built into the process. A couple of extra seconds before this one goes and the next one comes. Sometimes, in that space where nothing is supposed to happen, he used to take off his glove and press his palm flat against the glass or the body. Then he'd pull away quickly and watch the print flash up clear and detailed. A perfect outline of his hand visible for one second against the new paint or the dark tint, even the individual grooves of his thumb coming through. Whenever he did that, he used to imagine a detective. A smart person, somewhere far away, working with a magnifying glass and a light and a fine brush, dusting for clues. He used to imagine a person who could trace this car all the way back to him, back to this spot and this moment. A detective who could follow the chain of material evidence and find all the linkages and establish an incontrovertible proof.

The pay and the benefits are all that anybody else ever talks about and most of what they say is wrong. Massive inflation in all their numbers. Anti-union spin. He has done the real comparisons, added everything up and come out slightly ahead. To make the real money, you need to understand the complexity of the system and you need to think about taxes and shifting brackets. You need to figure out how to live with the overtime and how to get in there for the stat holidays.

When the kids were small, he used to scramble for the possibility of a double-time shift or for the perfect conditions that came around twice a year on Good Friday or Christmas.

It is more difficult to calculate the value of the benefits. The kids' braces and top-of-the-line Green Shield for their prescriptions. The education fund. He marched for those things. They walked arm in arm carrying the banner. Campaigned for the need to make progress, to look out for working families, to stand up against the big guys. Ken and Buzz and Bob making their speeches. A union puts you inside of something larger. Tickets for Tiger games and a rented bus. Tickets to the Wings and the Spitfires. Everyone sitting in the same section. All the good money his daughter picked up working TPT – Temporary Part-Time – in the summer. The card tournaments. The Christmas party and the Christmas bonus. The employee incentive plan. It was impossible to say no to the deal they gave you if you just bought what you built. Straight out of Henry Ford and the original Model T. Make enough to drive what you make. Four in a row. They went through four different vans before the last one. Hundreds of thousands of miles piled up. The kids grew up riding back there. It was their sole means of transportation.

*

He remembers turning around and telling the boy to shut up. The only clear part left. Hand on the wheel, craning his neck around. Looking at him closely. Wife sleeping in the passenger seat. Daughter already away at school.

His son. The teenage slacker called up from central casting. Lying down sideways in the back seat, high-tops up against the window. Head on the armrest. Game Boy. Ear

phones. Distortion coming out of his head. Tight jeans.
Black hooded sweatshirt. Hair in his eyes.

What a kid can do to a parent. A wave of disappointment
washing through him as he drives. Bitterness, like the taste of
ammonia, coursing through his mouth and his entire blood-
stream. He feels it in his feet. It has been nothing but continuous argument for months. The boy talking even though he
can't hear his own voice through the music. How it all sucks.
His parents are hypocrites. They say one thing and do
another. Smart teenager with bad grades and stupid friends.
Comes home one day with an idiot tattoo on his shoulder
blade. A tide of complaint that will not stop. How he doesn't
want to be here. How this is stupid. How he's going to run
away. How he's going to move out the minute, the minute,
he turns sixteen. You think you own me. You don't own me.

They cannot make him understand why it is important for
a family to do the same thing every year. Why you have to
hold on to your little traditions. It's only one day, his mother
says. A trip to the county in the fall. Follow the Number
Three and go to Ruthven. Joe Colosanti's Tropical Garden
and then Jack Miner's Bird Sanctuary. Plants and birds.
Muck and Cluck, his wife used to call it. Maybe this weekend
we'll go for the muck and cluck. What do you say?

At Colosanti's Tropical Garden they will sell you a minia-
ture cactus in its own clay pot for two dollars. Get the one
with the purple head. It can live on nothing. Push your finger against the needles for fun. There is no threat from a
Colosanti's cactus. It is what the kids will remember. The
greenhouses. The turtles and a little alligator swimming in
its pond. The humidity and the baby animals wandering
around, goats and chickens. They will remember that you
have to keep your palm flat when you feed an apple to a
pony.

Then on to Miner's. Every year the same thing. Canadian Geese by the thousands returning to Crazy Jack. A hundred years of banding and tracing routes and charting schedules. A warmer fall means a later departure. It doesn't take long. You drive by and it's over. You hear and you smell. The sound and the stink: incessant honking and acres of bird shit. That is what you get from a visit to Jack Miner's.

But there is something else, too. Something a person has to see at least once. The way an entire field can take off at the same time. The land deciding to become the sky. Everything lifting at once. Tight formations and instinctive patterns. That V writing itself on the clouds. You look at that and you don't forget you saw it. It can make you believe in order if you are the kind of person who wants to believe in order.

He remembers turning around and telling the boy to shut up. Last words. I'm getting so sick of your bullshit. Watch, he said. You watch. A couple of years down the road, you'll be thanking us for this.

Turning back, he catches a glimpse of his face as it passes the rear-view. The sneer. An angry man caught in a bit of glass. The red glint of the brake light comes through first, starts in the corner of his eye, then straight ahead. The back end of the flatbed. Too close. Already there. No chance to slow down. He tries to swerve, but they hit full tilt. Then rolling. They are strapped inside a rolling metal object. The V6 with 251 hp – a fire burning in the middle of a metal cube – the new fuel injection system. The driver's side airbag explodes out of the steering wheel, knocking him back against his chair. The back of his head slams into the rest. Bad twist in his neck. Sharp pain and an instant numbness in his legs. Powder burning in his eyes. His vision blurs. It happens fast but he sees it slowly before the total black comes down.

Two seconds worth of action is more than enough to fill in all the rest of the time that follows.

The airbags on her side do not deploy. The bags on the whole right-hand side of the vehicle do not deploy. They do not do what they are meant to do. Instead, they sit patient and useless, like a pile of neatly folded white towels in a linen closet.

Almost no visible change in her body. She is sleeping before her head goes against the window frame. Too hard. He knows it. The unnatural angle of her neck. The end of his wife. The way her ear moves too far to the side and her chin hangs too far down. One beat later, something flying past, about the size of a black hockey bag, thrown through the side window. He watches it move, following a smooth trajectory, an arc in the sky. That movement is the last thing he sees. It can't be processed. Elegant, he thinks, or something like that. The curve in the air.

*

Two days later he wakes up in the hospital. Can't feel his legs. His daughter holding his hand. She looks thin. His first thought. You need to eat more. Take better care of yourself.

There are six airbags in the Dodge Grand Caravan. Standard equipment, even on the base model. Safety sells. Front, side, and rear impact zones. They were the first to make it to market with protection like that. Went from design to production in an eighteen-month turnaround and caught everyone by surprise. Brought a little momentum back into sales. The car met or exceeded all standards set by the National Highway Transportation Safety Association. New sensors woven into the bumpers and the panels and the doors.

Scored above average on all the tests. You watch the crash test videos and see what you see. Those are the standard factory models.

In the videos it all works. Everything and every time. The bumper touches the test obstacle – the same immovable cube for all vehicles – and the bags deploy. Long before structural damage. Long before the crumpling of the frame dissipates and redirects the force of the impact. The dummies inside get tossed around. Sturdy back coils of spring in their necks wobble back and forth. Their fibreglass arms and legs extend, but you can tell they are going to be okay. If they were alive they would be okay. Everything behaves as it should. The touch on the bumper, the explosion of compressed gas inside the cabin. No hard surfaces left. No space at all. Nowhere to move. The vehicle becomes a solid mass. A wrecked exterior with a safe place at its core.

An electrical short, he figures. One circuit. A single wire that did not carry current the way it is supposed to. Failure of design or manufacture or installation. Everything is possible. Corrosion, perhaps. Not enough consideration made for the deteriorating affects of road salt. The back of the flatbed too high. Again, not standard. Higher than the test cube. The boy's unbuckled seatbelt. Nothing anybody could have done about that. A flaw outside of everything else. Mentioned in all the reports. Passengers are rarely thrown from a moving vehicle when seatbelts are used properly. Cops and their cameras. Images of everything. Pictures you shouldn't be allowed to take. A stranger's finger pushing down on a button. Numbered evidence. Accident recreation teams. Investigations. Measuring tapes. Insurance people with their duplicate sets of forms. The length of skid marks. Indexed to tread wear. The angle of impact. Angle the car left the road. They work backwards with their calculations. Crumple zones. Vectors.

Radius of broken glass. Distance from the car to the body in the field.

Twelve weeks in the hospital. Then twenty weeks of physio after that. The benefits covered everything and an officer at the Local made sure the paperwork moved along and the claims were filed on time. He had to learn to walk again, how to wiggle his toes, make his bowels churn on command. He lost almost half his weight and his hands callused against the railings. Messages sent from his brain and only slowly received. Twitching toes, half-bent knees, hips that took months before they remembered how to work right.

There was a moment to choose. An opening that wouldn't last long they said. Everybody talking about the same things. The Big Three going down. For real this time. Bankrupt and bailed out. Negotiations and concessions. The new deal and its different terms. Never going to be like it was before. Peak oil. Calculations that depended on the shifting value of a Mexican peso. Rising interest rates. The Environmental Protection Agency. Californian emission targets. Household debt levels. Burning wells in the Middle East. Security for a pipeline in Nigeria. Drilling in the arctic. What the average person in India does in their spare time. They said it all mattered.

He wasn't sure how it fit together, but when Essex Engine went down and the Foundry disappeared, he'd paid attention. When the fire in the Foundry went out for good – after burning for sixty years or whatever – that was important news. Ford guys told him that when they pulled the plug on the Foundry, even when they cut it off, the smelter burned hot for another week all by itself, with no external source of power, like a star, like the sun, generating its own heat and living on its own internal explosions. Then they went in with the heavy artillery and tore the whole thing down. You go to the Foundry now and it's gone.

A visitor sitting in the chair in his hospital room said, If they could get rid of us all and start again, that's what they'd do. You know that, right? That's what I'd do anyway. If I was in their shoes? I'd blow up the whole goddamn operation and blank slate it. Get all younger people to come in for less and do more. A fucking mess is what it is. Big fucking mess.

He signed as quickly as he could. Scribbled his name on the line and wrote the date like it was yesterday. You wait till it happens to you and see which way you go. Only an idiot says no to a buyout. Need to consider the facts. The numbers the company will put down to make you go away. This much to come to work tomorrow and tomorrow like usual. Or this much to stay home. You add in the pension, the best in the business, the RRSP's, the insurance, and the value of a big empty house. You get a figure. He read the statements, the digits and the commas spreading out beside his name. Couldn't quite catch the full meaning. Everything, everywhere in the world is falling apart, but he is okay. It will be like the depression they say, 30 percent unemployment and food rations, but it never comes. He has more than enough, more than he will ever need. Money like a foreign language he used to know but doesn't understand anymore.

*

After they cut his body out of the wreckage and lifted him away, he never touched the car again. The insurance company wrote the thing off as a totalled vehicle and he wondered what that meant. The total seemed like a raw number completely added up, the figure they reach for when they need to make something go away. He imagined the end of the van's life. Thought about those compacted cubes of metal he'd seen on TV and about the conveyors and the cranes and the incinerators at Zalev Brothers. He'd looked through the fence there once and watched the smokestacks and the bulldozers moving their mountains of ore. An unmaking as systematic as manufacture. It scared him. Metal turned back into a ferrous dust and smoke. The remains of 12 million Magic Wagons absorbed into the ground, secreted into the river, or floating in the sky to become a microscopic coating of ash inside your lungs.

The same transformations for us, he thinks. A person is one thing and one thing and one thing. Then he is something else. There is a pivot, a before and an after, a shifting. The day he decided to take the buyout. That was it for him. Not the accident. Not the day he left the hospital or the week when his daughter went back to her own life. Not even today, the day she forgot. Everything else is second to the moment when he decided to really walk away, to move exclusively under his own power. Walk and never drive again. Walk and not even allow himself to be carried in another car or taxi or bus. This was the one connection he needed to break. His life fused to the internal combustion engine, almost since the beginning. He wanted them not to touch anymore.

It has been almost a year now and he thinks he has managed it well enough. The groceries and the doctor's appointments and the bank. He leaves himself plenty of time and is never late. Follows a regular routine. A network of well-worn paths through his contracted orbit and a different way of understanding the city. He has his short cuts and his tangents, places he doesn't go anymore. It has been doable so far, but this will be something different. The map says it is thirty miles.

Before he goes to bed, he packs his bag. A raincoat, just in case, and different layers for the way the temperature shifts during the day. A stack of six sandwiches and a water bottle. He sets the alarm for 5:30 and puts his head against the pillow. Then he gets up again and goes down to the kitchen. Digs out a flashlight and some extra batteries. It is going to be dark, he reminds himself. It will be dark at the beginning and the end.

University to Huron Church. Huron Church all the way out to the fork where the 401 begins and the Number Three branches off. Then follow the Number Three to the spot. He will know it when he gets there. The way is simple, a long diagonal cut. University to Huron Church to the Number Three. He repeats it as he falls asleep. It will take all day. Even if he starts early, it will take the full day, but he will get there. He will be where he needs to be.

In the morning, he wakes ahead of the alarm. Gets up and eats another egg and even washes the pan and his plate. He pulls on a toque and a pair of gloves, and shrugs a backpack over his shoulders before reaching for the doorknob. Outside, his breath fogs against the darkness and he turns and squeezes a note into the space between the door and the frame. If she checks, she will know where to find him. He turns the key and slips it into his pocket.

In the early stages, it goes faster than he expected. The longer distance he has to cover makes his normal routes seem shorter. The left leg is worse than the right – he cannot bend it enough to ride a bike – but the humidity is not bad and once he warms up, he finds a regular stride and moves steadily. University passes quickly before he makes the turn onto Huron Church. The spire of Assumption and the old buildings of the school stand on his left across from the massive concrete foundations of the bridge on his right. There is only one block left meant for people and even that is fading as everything clears out to make way for the second span. This is the issue of the day. A second bridge and where it will go and what it will mean and what it will cost and who will pay. Politicians and businessmen arguing on both sides of the border. They say the traffic demands a second span and that it must go here or it must go there. The single most important crossing on the continent, the lifeline of two economies. Delays that must be stopped. The flow of goods over the line. Free Trade and the Autopact. They repeat and repeat. The traffic demands a second span. The traffic demands a second span, as though traffic sets its own course free of human interference. He thinks of the twisted arms and the faces pushed up against the wall and the backroom payouts. Boarded-up houses on Indian road where his kids' friends used to live. All of them gone now, purposely flooded and left to rot until demolition is the only option. It is hard for him to even look at it. Almost like the other side, he thinks. Almost as bad as Detroit itself.

He moves on and the Caravan follows him everywhere. Parked along the curb and sleeping in driveways and overnight lots, idling at the McDonald's pick-up window and blinking in the left-turn lane. It is always close by, bumper humming just six inches from his repaired knee as he passes inside the crosswalk. Every make and model. Some twelve or fifteen years old, rumbling by, exhaling exhaust and pulling in the air. He can see what the drivers don't know. Those struts are done, my friend. All the ninety-eights had the same problem. And that hint of rust around the wheel well? Looks like nothing right now, but wait one year. Should have sprung for the metallic paint. The telltale wobbles. The bad alignments and the burning oil. The faulty ignitions and the squealing timing belts. Bald tires and bad brakes. He remembers the big radiator recall.

After Wyandotte, after he passes beneath the bridge, the American-bound transports take over. A person walking in this place takes matters into his own hands. The toll plaza and the duty free. The University Stadium, the High School. Two different malls. The strip bar and the fast food. The motels and the fruit stands. They all rise in front and he walks them down. Six lanes running on his right. Trucks backed up and waiting. Petunias planted in the middle of a median strip.

He takes a break at the cloverleaf where Huron Church passes under the Expressway. Six lanes running full tilt on the ground and four more running perpendicular over his head. A place that makes its own air currents. He sits on the hill, eats a sandwich and feels good about his progress. Watches the newspapers and plastic bags swirling always in the same pattern. Sucked upwards and sideways. After the expressway, there are houses with neat hedges set back from the road and then Saint Clair College and the outlet centres and cemeteries lined up on the right. Heavenly Rest waits near the junction where the 401 begins and ends and the Number Three branches off. His wife and his son are in there and it has all been paid for, but he has never seen the graves and cannot stop now to check. The daylight needs to be preserved.

As he moves along the Number Three, he thinks about all the other times he came this way before the accident. There are only two lanes and he remembers how the slower drivers used to frustrate him. It was always easy enough to blow by one of them, but impossible if you ever got stuck behind two or three in a row, especially at night. The way he used to stare at the speedometer and announce the pace. Sixty-three kilometres an hour, he'd say. Sixty-three. Are they all going to church? And he'd gesture through the windshield and calculate the risk of a sudden passing attempt. How fast he'd have to go and how long he'd have to spend on the wrong side of a busy road. He usually took his shot because he trusted the guts of the van. How surprisingly nimble it could be if he had to pick it up for a short burst. He'd hit the signal and drive his foot to the floor and swerve out over the dotted line to take down four stragglers in one go before cutting back to avoid a head-on collision. Whenever they were out there on the wrong side, his wife used to put her hand out and touch his chest and tell him to go back. Stop it, she'd say. Stop it. You know I don't like this. You're going to get us all killed for nothing.

As he walks along the shoulder, he faces the traffic and tries to make eye-contact with each driver. He thinks about all the other kinds of accidents. The big hundred-car pileup that shut down the whole 401 for a week. That wasn't far from here. A diesel fire that burned so hot it melted the road down to the bare earth and welded all the cars together. And all the little side-swipes and fender-benders and the rigs that end up wrapped around hydro poles or flipped on their backs with their wheels spinning in the air. You can count on a car accident. The next one and the next one and the next one. Steady and reliable and always arriving on schedule and in the same places. Rush hour and the dark drunk interval between one and four in the morning. The night after the prom. The poorly engineered curve and the bad intersection and the nasty stretch between Chatham and the Bridge. Ask a 9-1-1 operator, ask the person who dispatches the cops and the ambulance. She will tell you. Nothing surprising ever happens on her regular shift.

He can't walk twenty minutes on the Number Three without seeing another homemade memorial. The white wooden crosses – three feet high and hung with faded artificial flowers – are almost as frequent as kilometre markers. He pulls himself in and out of the ditches and reads every one. Dates and ages scribbled in black. Some are impossible and faded and some are twenty-years-old and still bright. He thinks of the hand coming back to re-paint and re-write the same words every spring and fall. People holding on to their rituals. There are vases and ragged teddy bears and laminated photographs and small piles of rocks that can't be random.

After the high heat of the afternoon, his head begins to feel fuzzy and a sunburn cracks his lips. The last of his water is gone and he knows he must be a little dehydrated, but he recognizes the spot immediately. It is impossible to make a mistake when you approach this gradually. The traces of tread are still there and they point the way, directing him back. He steps clearly into what passed so quickly the first time and everything is as it was. He thinks he can almost see the space he opened in last year's corn. He goes in, parts the stalks like coats on a rack. From the road, the field looks scattered, but inside everything is straight and the rows are evenly planted. It is all the space he needs.

Good, he says. Good enough. He lies down with them. Palms flat on the ground and his cheek turned. This is what he came to do. The shadow from a cloud passes over and a tide of deep fatigue rises. Dizziness and a regular throbbing in his legs now that he has stopped. There is no next move. He rests his head on the backpack and closes his eyes. One quiet hour here with them. A bit of time spent together and then he will head back. Maybe he will get a motel on the way home.

His body rests in the cornfield and a crowd of stalks stands over him. Waning sunlight, green warmth, insects and silence. An ant crawling on the back of his hand. Mosquitoes and then a single Monarch butterfly. Almost time for you to go, he thinks. He remembers a visit to Point Pelee, something the guide said about their incredible migration. The amount of time it takes to make it down to Mexico every year, their repeating cycles and the long distances and short lifespans. Four rounds before they get through. Whole generations born and giving out while still en route.

There is a whirring when he opens his eyes. He hears the road but can't see it. It is dark and cold and he is stiff. His watch says 8:30 but the night is already full black. More than four hours of sleep and he is still exhausted. He tries to stand but his joints feel calcified and arthritic. A swollen knee and puffy fluid he can squeeze through his jeans. Tough going from here . Need to be careful and take it easy. He limps out of the field and up the ditch. Grabs at a tangle of grass to get some leverage. There is a pain in his foot when he pushes off and something wrong with his breathing, a soreness behind his ear. He emerges onto the shoulder and crosses over.

A single ray of light cuts the dark and comes down on him fast. He hears a high-pitched drone and watches the light approach. There is nothing reflective on his body and the kid is almost on top of him before he sees and makes his adjustment. There is a quick cut away from the side and a fading waaaaaaaaah. He catches only the first syllable of the boy swearing at him. Ninety miles an hour, he thinks, at least. Wearing only a billowing T-shirt and a pair of jeans. Skinny arms and bare elbows and his legs wrapped around the engine of a purple Kawasaki. A yellow helmet with a fire decal, streak of colour in the night. Maybe a hundred, he reconsiders. That kid might be moving a hundred miles an hour.

He keeps the flashlight pointed at his feet and walks with one foot on the asphalt and one foot on the gravel. There is a white line that separates the road from everything else and he tries to follow it, but the pavement crumbles in spots and comes apart. He turns his back and pushes his palm against his eyes whenever a car approaches. Needs to keep his pupils from dilating if he wants to hold his night vision. There are no stars in the sky and he remembers a smog warning from the forecast, high rates of particulate matter in the air.

He is not certain if this is the right direction anymore. Could be mixed-up and turned around and moving out instead of back. There is wetness in his socks and dryness in his mouth. He thinks there must be one sandwich left, but it isn't in the bag. Should have brought more water. He feels himself weaving across the line, but can't adjust in time and comes back too far, rolls his ankle, and falls into a swampy culvert. People with their high beams on and the slipstream from every passing vehicle. Always this wind knocking him around. The biggest trucks create a vacuum that takes everything away, even the air. He has no idea how long he has been out here.

It would be easier to stop and take three steps to the left. He knows this. No one would be surprised. Just time it right and close his eyes and move laterally and open his arms. He could wait for the next Plymouth Voyager. Select the one he wants, identify its approaching headlights and press himself against the oncoming grill. He could feel the sails of the ship and sink all the way through. Penetrate directly to the core and meld with the moving parts. The option is always there.

Another pair of lights rises up, but they seem different and more threatening. The beams aim and come directly and the horn wails from too far out. He covers his eyes and turns his back. Hears the tires as they hit the gravel. He makes himself small. Crouches. Feels the skidding up through the ground. There is a hot smell of exhaust and burning rubber. He puts his chin on his knees and waits for the blow, but it doesn't come. A door opens and slams shut. He hears footsteps and sees a darkness in front of the light. Then a hand sweeping his face, fingers on his cheek. The voice from the telephone. A weak connection, but the signal coming through. I'm here, she says.

Fresh water pouring over his head. She puts the bottle to his mouth. You need to drink. Drink this.

His eyes adjust. She is coming back and, at first, he is not sure if this is real. It could be a stranger, just another person in a car. Perhaps he is making himself see something. It takes a second before he knows. She is there and it is true. He puts both his hands on her shoulders, tests it, and then transfers some of his weight over.

Where have you been? she yells at him. There is no apology in her voice. The forgotten phone call happened years ago. Her eyes are bright and scared and she is spitting the words.

I've been going back and forth on this road for hours. You know that? Just looking and looking and hoping I'd find you before something happened. Driving past that same spot again and again. I didn't know what you'd do out here by yourself. I almost called the police, Dad. You almost made me call the police.

She pulls her hands through her hair and looks far off to the side. The cars roar by and each one makes her wince. She seems exhausted. Older than he remembers from the last time.

She leads him over to her car, engine still running.

Get in, she says, and she opens the door. We need to go home. We need to get you into a bed.

She waves her hand into the space at the passenger's side but he will not enter. He is standing in the mouth of the car, the V between the open door and the interior, and he tells her no. Tells her he won't.

A motel, he says. How much farther? The idea is there, but the words slur a little. A motel in Essex. I need to get there. Just for tonight. Then we see.

She shakes her head, no. No. We need to stop this right now, okay? I've been out here for hours and I want to go home. Please stop this. Just get in. Please get in. Please.

He hears a hint of alarm in her voice and knows she is trying to cover it up. She likely thinks he isn't right in the head anymore. Her hand goes to his shoulder and she pushes him down, tries to lower his body onto the seat.

He resists, feels his feet set hard on the ground. A sense of clarity returning and some strength. The shock of water helping. Everything is coming back to him now. Her hand on his shoulder. The right place at the right time and they are here together. This has always been the plan.

I am going to a motel tonight, he says. And you can come or you can go. Just tell me how much farther.

I don't know, she screams. How am I supposed to know? Why are you doing this? Maybe a couple of miles that way. Her hand waves in the dark. Let me bring you at least. It will take us five minutes.

The still moment of confrontation. They stand one foot apart on the side of the road. He sways from the ankles and she looks at his hair and his clothes and his feet. Streaks of filth running behind his ears and down his neck. She shakes her head, stares at the space between his eyes and then looks away. He can see it when she turns. A tremor moving through, the crack in this hard performance. Her cheeks flush and he watches the anger and frustration mix with something else he can recognize. There are things we must allow each other that have nothing to do with kindness.

This doesn't change anything, she says and she spreads both her arms wide as if to absorb the whole scene. A muscle ripples in her cheek. You know that, right? This won't change what you did.

She pushes the heels of her hands hard against her eye sockets and then she shakes her head again and leans over to kiss him on the cheek. She walks back to the car, puts it in gear, checks over her shoulder, and sweeps through a U-turn. When she pulls up beside him, she hits the hazards and he looks to her through the window. She flicks her wrist and waves him ahead and he nods and starts to walk. She follows with her tires rotating to match his pace, a half-turn at a time. The four-ways flash and her headlights shine up on his back. He walks on the shoulder, then on the side, then in the middle of the lane and his shadow stretches out in front, the outline of a human body cast down onto the pavement, but still moving. Other cars come up from behind, slow down and almost crawl. There is a moment of confusion, a pause. A string of red tail lights extends back into the darkness and the whole strange parade inches forward.

Acknowledgements

Several of these stories appeared in slightly different forms in the following journals: *The Fiddlehead*, *The Notre Dame Review*, *Exile* and *The New Quarterly*. I want to thank the editors of these publications, especially Kim Jernigan at *TNQ*, for their support. Dennis Priebe did a wonderful job with the design and typesetting of the collection and the whole team at Biblioasis worked very hard on this book. I received arts grants from The Canada Council and The Nova Scotia Ministry of Tourism and Culture and I gratefully acknowledge these contributions.

Thanks to my family for showing the way along this 'road we must walk.' And appreciation, also, to the Garrett, Ryall, Gervais, and McCormack clans. A special, very deep, reservoir of gratitude is saved for my friends: Jason and Jason, Rich, Drew, Mark, Jere, Michel, and Seán. Saint Mary's University has been a great place to work. My colleagues at the school, especially Brian Bartlett, have been inspirational and our students have taught me a lot about how to read (and maybe even write) a story.

Three people helped me with this collection in ways that merit special recognition. Dan Wells called the book into being and, in all the important ways, *Light Lifting* is our shared labour. His keen editorial eye saved me on several occasions and he has cared for and about these stories in ways that I can't ever repay and will never forget. Harold Hoefle read and re-read every word and scribbled and spidered his way across every page. He and I are in it for the long haul and his talent, generosity and brute diligence have already carried me over many miles. My wife, Crystal Garrett, is responsible for most of what is good in here and none of what is bad. Her journalist's mind cuts always to the core and her gut feelings should always be trusted. The day we met was the luckiest day of my life.

About the Author

Alexander MacLeod was born in Inverness, Cape Breton and raised in Windsor, Ontario. His award-winning stories have appeared in many of the leading Canadian and American journals and have been selected for *The Journey Prize Anthology*. He holds degrees from the University of Windsor, the University of Notre Dame, and McGill. He currently lives in Dartmouth, Nova Scotia and teaches at Saint Mary's University in Halifax.